A Glory of Unicorns

COMPILED BY
Bruce Coville

ILLUSTRATED BY
Alix Berenzy

SCHOLASTIC PRESS
NEW YORK

Compilation copyright © 1998 by Bruce Coville. Illustrations copyright © 1998 by Alix Berenzy. All rights reserved. Published by Scholastic Press, a division of Scholastic Inc. *Publishers since 1920.* SCHOLASTIC and SCHOLASTIC PRESS and associated logos are trademarks or registered trademarks of Scholastic Inc.

Library of Congress Cataloging-in-Publication Data

A glory of unicorns / edited by Bruce Coville.
p.   cm.
Summary: Twelve short stories, by such authors as Nancy Varian
Berberick, Gregory Maguire, and Katherine Colville, about unicorns in
both mythical and contemporary settings.
ISBN 0-590-95943-3
1. Children's stories, American.   [1. Unicorns — Juvenile fiction.
2. Unicorns — Fiction.   3. Short stories.]   I. Coville, Bruce.
PZ5.G497   1998
[Fic] — dc21   97-13689
CIP
AC

2   4   6   8   10   9   7   5   3   1

Printed in the U.S.A.
First printing, May 1998
Design by David Caplan

for Norlynn McMullen

ONTENTS

A GATHERING, A GLORY

It is a game among people who love words to come up with appropriate terms for groups of animals (or humans, for that matter). Thus we speak not only of a herd of cows or a gaggle of geese, but also a pride of lions, a knot of toads, and a quarrel of lawyers.

To this list I propose a new addition: A Glory of Unicorns.

Of course, one unicorn is glorious in and of itself. But when you have several of them together—well, that is something else indeed, a thought (or a sight, should you be so lucky) to lift the heart and make it sing.

A glory.

Why this should be so is an interesting matter. I know that I have loved the idea of unicorns for as long as I can remember, imagined them, dreamed of glimpsing one, or even better, befriending it. I know, too, that I am not alone in this, since wherever I go I meet fellow unicorn lovers.

But why is this so? Why do so many of us yearn for unicorns? After all, in this fast-paced, high-tech world, there wouldn't seem to be much room for such beasts. Yet you find images of them everywhere, on posters and coasters, coffee mugs and greeting cards. You can buy them shaped from crystal or pewter or ceramic, rearing back or resting, galloping, flying, soaring.

My guess is that we seek them not merely for their beauty, even though they are more than beautiful enough. I think they call to our hearts so strongly because they represent something sadly lost; their very presence sings of the ancient wonder pervading the natural world, a sense of wonder hard to hold in these modern times. Underlying our desire for unicorns, I suspect, is a longing for purity, a memory of magic, an aching need to recover innocence. In their horns, their eyes, their very being, they carry the hope of healing, the promise of grace.

But beware! That wonder and that healing and that grace do not come without a price, as many of these stories will tell you. For this is not a book about sappy unicorns. The writers of the stories that follow know magic is tough, love hard and demanding, and unicorns not as easy as some of us might like to think; neither safe, nor sweet, nor simple. Following the unicorn path requires all the strength, patience, and courage you can muster. Unicorns expect sacrifice from those who love them—and from those they love in return.

But if your heart is bold and your spirit true, the rewards can be great indeed.

Downright glorious, in fact.

So take a deep breath and turn the page.

You'll find a glory of unicorns, waiting to sweep you away.

The
Guardian
of Memory

— BRUCE COVILLE —

(*A tale from* THE UNICORN CHRONICLES)

The banging at the door woke Grimwold, keeper of the Unicorn Chronicles, from his nap.

Naturally, this made the old dwarf even more crotchety than usual, and he grumbled mightily as he headed down the long, wood-paneled tunnel that led to the outside world.

The banging continued.

"I'm coming!" he shouted as he stumped along. "I'm *coming*!"

More banging. He could tell from the sound that it was made by a hoof.

"Bang, bang, bang," he muttered. "Dratted nuisance anyway." When he finally reached the door he yanked it open and snarled, "Well, what do *you* want?"

The unicorn standing outside looked slightly startled. Speaking respectfully, he said, "It is time for the changing of the guard. The queen sent us to escort you to the ceremony."

"Well there's no need to kick the door down! I was just getting my things ready. Come in while I finish." He glanced past the unicorn and sighed. Four others stood waiting behind the one he had been speaking to.

"You can *all* come in," he grumbled.

Quietly, on hooves that could cross a field of flowers without bending a stem, the glory of unicorns entered Grimwold's underground home. They passed through the door like a sudden surge of moonlight, manes and tails shimmering, horns like spears made of pearl and ice.

"I'll be with you in a moment," said Grimwold.

Padding back through the lantern-lit tunnel, past the paintings of unicorns and mermaids and humans who had played a part in Luster's history, the dwarf made his way through the story room to the Chronicles themselves. Going to one of the oldest of the wooden racks, he selected the proper scroll—though it was hardly necessary, since he knew the story he had to tell by heart.

He stopped in his living quarters long enough to grab a fresh robe and splash some water on his face, then returned to the waiting unicorns.

"You're Dreamhorn," he said, looking at the leader. "Son of Ayla Forestfriend."

Dreamhorn nodded. "You keep good track of us."

"Have to," muttered Grimwold. "Queen insists. Well, what are we waiting for? If I have to do this, I have to. Let's get going."

Dreamhorn looked toward the others and nodded.

They started back through the door, which Grimwold had not bothered to close earlier.

The little man was the last to leave. He pulled the door shut behind him, sighed, then climbed onto Dreamhorn's back. Riding a unicorn was supposed to be a great honor. Grimwold, however, preferred to walk, and rode now only because he was too old to travel the entire distance to the gathering place on foot—a fact that annoyed him no end.

Grimwold and the unicorns journeyed peacefully, with no sign of the delvers that were the unicorns' main enemy in Luster. Autumn was on the land, the forest rich with the reds and oranges of the season. The wind moved occasionally through the fallen leaves, stirring and rustling them. The unicorns' silver hooves made no sound at all.

At the end of the third day they reached the gathering place, a large grotto where a high waterfall tumbled into a silver pool. Not all the unicorns of Luster were required to attend the ceremony; even this place could not hold that many of them. But there would be a good number of them—including all who might be chosen to become the new Guardian of Memory.

Though they arrived two days before the ceremony was scheduled to take place, Arabella Skydancer, Queen of the Unicorns, was there to greet them.

Grimwold closed his eyes for a moment when he spotted the queen. It hurt him to see how thin his old friend had become. Not thin in the sense of gaunt or bony. Her thinness was that of one who was fading away. Though he would not want to admit it out loud, Grimwold knew he would miss her when she left this world behind.

The queen bowed her head in greeting when she saw him enter the grotto. Grimwold returned the gesture, fighting down a surge of emotion as he remembered all they had been through together over the years, the dangers they had faced, the boons she had granted him in return for his service.

"The time has come again," she said softly, when he was standing by her side.

"As it always does," said Grimwold. "All too swiftly."

"Not too swiftly for the current Guardian," said the queen, sounding amused.

Grimwold nodded. Though it had been twenty-five years since the last changing of the guard, he remembered the ceremony vividly, and the sorrow that had followed when Night Eyes was chosen. Manda Seafoam, his mother, had been nearly inconsolable. But then, someone always mourned when the Guardian was chosen.

"You have been well?" asked the queen, interrupting his thoughts.

"Well enough."

"And busy?"

"Too busy. If your subjects would stop having adventures for a year or two, I might be able to catch up on my work. As it is, Arabella, I fear I shall never be current."

The queen laughed, a sound like water on smooth stones, like wind passing through daisies. Grimwold had been making the same complaint for over two hundred years.

"I'll see what I can do," she said.

The dwarf snorted, which is not considered an appropriate response to the queen. Arabella pretended not to hear.

He was woken the next morning by a unicorn standing at the foot of his bed. She made no sound, simply glared at him. But the old dwarf felt her presence, even in his sleep.

Opening one eye, he glared back at the unicorn and growled, "Leave me alone."

"I have to speak to you," she said urgently.

With an exasperated sigh, Grimwold sat up. "About what? Not a story, I hope. I don't take stories this early in the morning. Lots of others ahead of you, anyway."

The unicorn shook her head. "I want you to tell me how I can be chosen to be the next Guardian."

Grimwold blinked in astonishment. "Have you been drinking moonbeams? No one *wants* that job. Do you have any idea how appalling it is?" He narrowed his eyes. "Who are you, anyway?"

The unicorn started to answer, but Grimwold raised his hand. "Wait, let me figure it out. Never saw you before, but I know that flow of mane. The horn—yes, the horn would be . . . Turn around!"

The unicorn did as asked, making a full circle for the dwarf.

Grimwold snorted in triumph. "You're Cloudmane,

daughter of Streamstrider. The queen is your grand-mother."

The unicorn's large eyes widened in astonishment. "How did you do that?"

"It's my job to keep track of you unicorns—even young and foolish ones like you. Now, why in the world do you want to be chosen Guardian? Oh, never mind. It doesn't make any difference anyway, you silly thing. Only stallions take that job. It's not for mares. And a good thing—dangerous, thankless task that it is." He narrowed his eyes. "Why *do* you want the job? Out to prove some-thing? Running away? Some young stallion break your heart?"

Cloudmane's nostrils flared, and her enormous blue eyes flashed with a fire and a strength that surprised the old dwarf. "My reasons are my own," she snapped, her mane bristling. "I ask only for some advice."

"Then I'll give you some. And I hope you'll take it. Forget the whole idea. The job of Guardian is not for you —not for any unicorn in its right mind. It's not a job you volunteer for, it's a job you take only because you have no choice."

"We'll see about that," muttered Cloudmane. Spin-ning on her silver hooves she trotted away, her seafoam tail whisking angrily behind her. She made not a sound as she crossed the carpet of dried leaves that covered the for-est floor.

Grimwold closed his eyes and tried to go back to sleep, but it was impossible. The rising sun was too bright, the conversation too upsetting. And he missed the comforts of his familiar caves. Feeling even crankier than usual, he rose and went to the stream to get a drink and wash his face.

All through the day, as the unicorns arrived Grimwold fretted about his conversation with Cloudmane and wondered if he should speak of it to the queen. But Arabella was busy with her duties. Between preparing for the ceremony and greeting old and honored friends, she had little enough time for him to bother her with nonsense from a young mare that, in the end, would come to nothing anyway.

Many of the arriving unicorns made it a point to seek out Grimwold. Some came to tell him they had new adventures for him to record in the Chronicles. Others wanted simply to greet him and to inquire after his health —a kindness that pleased the old dwarf in spite of himself.

He kept an eye out for Cloudmane, but did not see her again.

Aside from Grimwold, only a handful of two-legs were invited to the ceremony. One was a girl named Ivy, who had the queen's blessing. Another was a painter named Master Chang, a handsome man with brown eyes and long, dark hair who sometimes made pictures of important events in Luster, pictures that were stored with Grimwold in the Cavern of the Chronicles. A third was Madame Leonetti, an old woman who wore a dark blue robe and gazed out at the world from beneath its hood with eyes so sharp and bright it seemed they could start a fire of their own accord.

Ivy came to stand beside Grimwold as he was watching the unicorns gather. She fussed with her long red hair for a moment—the wind kept trying to rearrange it—then asked shyly, "Did you finish my story?"

Grimwold, who was no taller than the girl, gave her a sad look. "I have written down what happened to you so far. But it will be many years before your story is finished." *Many long, hard years,* he wanted to add. But he bit back the words.

Ivy nodded. "May I stand with you for a while?"

"It would be my pleasure," replied Grimwold. He was starting to feel nervous about the ceremony and his part in it, and was glad of a distraction.

After a while the dwarf and the girl climbed a narrow path that led to the top of the cliff over which the waterfall flowed. Evening passed softly into full night. Still standing together, high above the ceremonial ground, they continued to watch the unicorns gather.

It was like watching moonlight collect in a bowl, save that it seemed there were as many shades and tones of whiteness as there were stars burning in the vast, clear sky above them.

"Never this many at home," said Ivy, looking upward.

"Unicorns, or stars?" asked Grimwold.

"No unicorns at home at all," said Ivy sadly.

Grimwold snorted. "That's not quite true, my girl. What do you think this ceremony is about, after all?"

"I don't know."

He turned to her in surprise. "No one has told you?"

"The queen said I would find out in good time."

Grimwold hesitated, then said, "This may be as good a time as any."

"Are you going to tell me a story?" Ivy asked eagerly.

"Might as well. Have to tell it down there in a little while. Good warm-up to tell it to you now."

They walked along the edge of the cliff, going far enough from the waterfall so that Grimwold could speak without having to work to be heard above its sound. Ivy found a seat on a moss-covered rock. Grimwold stood before her and cleared his throat.

"You know, of course, that long ago the unicorns lived on Earth."

"Of course," said Ivy solemnly.

"And that they came here because they were hunted so ferociously that they were in danger of extinction."

"Yes," said Ivy sadly.

"But do you know what happened to your world after they left?"

She shook her head.

"Then I shall tell you."

The old dwarf closed his eyes for a moment. Ivy heard the flick of wings above her, the occasional cry of a nightbird, a rustling in the nearby bushes. When Grimwold finally began to speak his voice was deeper, softer, calmer than usual.

This is the tale he told her:

In the long ago and sweet of the world, when things were slower but hearts were no less fierce, there came a time when the unicorns had to leave.

This was not done easily, nor was it done without grief. Earth was home to the unicorns, and they were part of it, horn and mane and hoof. But to stay was to die, for the hunting of unicorns by their enemies had become all too successful.

Finally they fled here to Luster.

The passage was not an easy one, and more than one unicorn gave its life to help in the creation of the first door between the two worlds.

When the migration was over, and the last unicorn had left, it was as if the earth itself sighed with loss and sorrow.

For what is a world that has no unicorns?

That loss and that sorrow grew within the hearts of those who lived on Earth. Even those who had never seen a unicorn, never heard of a unicorn, felt the passing of something sweet and wonderful. It was as if the air had surrendered a bit of its spice, the water a bit of its sparkle, the night a bit of its mystery.

But only a very few knew why.

Not all felt the loss in equal measure. The coarse and the crude were but vaguely aware of something making them uneasy in their quiet moments. Most people simply felt a little sadder, a little wearier. But for those most open to the beauty of the world and all its joys and sorrows, there was an ache in the heart that grew greater by the day, until it seemed that grief would overwhelm them.

Painters painted only scenes of sorrow; singers and players now made only mournful music; storytellers, sensing the loss, told tales that made their audiences weep long into the night, and offered no light tales, no comedy, for relief.

Gloom enfolded the world.

And finally a child—it's always a child, you know— decided something had to be done.

She was the daughter of a storyteller, and seemed likely to become a storyteller herself. Her name was Alma, and she had a heart of steel and fire. She went to her brother, Balan, and said, "Something is wrong, and I am going to find out what. Will you travel with me, brother?"

And though Balan was more given to doing than to thinking, to fighting than to feeling, he agreed to go with his sister, for he did not want her to travel alone. She gathered some food and a few coins, which she carried in a pack on her back, and several of her father's best stories, which she carried in her heart, and set out. She went on foot, and Balan walked beside her, one hand on his sword.

And the sword was needed, for the road was perilous. It had always been dangerous, even in the best of times. But with the passing of the unicorns, hearts had become hungry, and in some that hunger had turned to viciousness.

For three years Alma and Balan traveled through peril and pain, and many times Balan's sword saved them from disaster, and many other times Alma's stories gained them food and shelter, and sometimes even a clue.

Finally, weak and weary, wandering through a deep forest, they came upon the home of an old magician named Bellenmore. It was set in the side of a hill, and magic hung thick about it. When they first approached the door it began to sing:

> *Bellenmore, Bellenmore!*
> *Wanderers two outside your door!*

Then a wall—or something like a wall, for they could not see it, only feel it—rose in front of them, and they could go no farther.

There they waited, until the old man appeared. Glaring at them from under bushy eyebrows, he said in a voice that creaked and cracked with age, "Well, what do you want?"

"We want to know what's gone wrong with the world," said Alma, her voice gentle, coaxing. "For three years now things have seemed flat and stale. Something is lost, and we have come seeking it."

Bellenmore closed his eyes, and released a sigh so heavy it seemed to flow not from his body but from someplace deep in the earth itself. "I was afraid of this."

"Of what?" asked Balan, struggling to raise his sword, which seemed frozen at his side.

"Of exactly what this girl—your sister, I assume from the look of her—has just described. The unicorns have gone, and when they left they took with them something that is essential to the human heart."

"The unicorns!" said Alma, with sudden understanding. "Where have they gone? And why? How did they get there? Can I follow them?"

"Hold, hold!" cried the old magician, raising his hands. "One question at a time."

He studied them for a moment, then made a small gesture with the little finger of his right hand. The invisible wall disappeared, and Balan gained control of his sword once more.

"You may come in," said Bellenmore.

Balan glanced at his sister. "Do you think it's safe?"

"Nothing is safe," she said sharply. Then she stepped forward, toward the old man, and followed him through the door into the hill.

The inside of his house was warm and cozy, and slightly strange. A green fire crackled on the hearth. On the mantel above the fireplace stood a row of earthenware mugs with hideous faces. One of them winked at Alma, another leered and rolled its eyes, and a third stuck out its tongue and made a rude noise. Then they all began to sing a bawdy song. Bellenmore waved a hand to silence them.

The tables and chairs were made of dark wood, and

ornately carved—some with odd designs, others with scenes of dragons and unicorns. At one side of the room was a tall oaken stand; a thick book rested open upon it. The longest table held a glass cage with no top. Inside the cage was a lizard, which was resting its front legs on the upper edge of the cage and staring out at them with a curious expression.

"Sit," said Bellenmore, gesturing toward one of the chairs.

Alma sat. Balan stood behind her, both because he had not been invited to sit, and because he would not have sat even had he been asked. His hand rested on the hilt of his sword.

Bellenmore did sit, his robe shifting and whispering around him as if it were alive.

"Alas, the unicorns," he said sadly.

"What happened to them?" asked Alma.

"They were driven away. There is a family that holds an ancient grudge against them, and the hunting had become so fierce that it seemed they all might perish. Finally the unicorn queen came to me and asked if I might open a door for them, as I had for the dragons."

"The dragons?" asked Balan, confused.

The magician shrugged. "It was much the same thing. The world is changing, boy. Wildness and magic are in retreat before the rise of men. Better—much better—it would be for science and magic, order and wildness, natural and supernatural to live together. But that cannot be, at least not for now. So the dragons have gone, and the unicorns had to leave as well. I helped them open a door to a place that they have named Luster. It is a good place for them. But they did take a piece of our hearts with them when they went."

"Send me through the door," said Alma.

The old man looked startled. "That's not possible."

"Why?"

Bellenmore blew a puff of air through his shaggy white mustache, then looked down at his knobby hands. Finally he said, "The queen wouldn't like it."

"I don't like what's happened here," replied Alma firmly. "I must speak to them."

"They are not tame beasts, you know."

"I am not a tame girl."

Bellenmore stood. "Come here, girl."

Alma rose from her chair and went to stand before the magician. He reached into the pocket of his robe and pulled forth a leather bag. "Here," he said. "Take this for your troubles."

The bag was very heavy. Alma undid the strings that held it shut and glanced inside.

It was filled with gold and jewels.

She snorted and handed it back to him. "Don't be silly. That's not what I came for."

A corner of his mouth twitched upward in what might have been a smile. "I guess it's not," he whispered. He looked at her for a moment longer, and she could tell that he was testing her again, even more than he had with the bag of gold, though she couldn't tell how.

Finally he sighed. "I have to get something," he said gruffly. "You stay there."

After she had nodded her agreement, he crossed to a door at the far side of the room. When he opened it and stepped through, he seemed to disappear into a kind of shadowy gloom. Balan started forward, but Alma shook her head. He resumed his stance behind her chair.

When Bellenmore returned he was holding a golden chain, from which dangled a crystal amulet. Inside the crystal was coiled a long strand of white hair that seemed to glow with a light all its own.

"This amulet was a gift of the queen," he said. "There are only five such in all the world. It will allow you to pass into the land of the unicorns."

Alma took it from him. It felt warm in her hand.

The magician leaned forward and in whispered tones told her how to use it. Her eyes grew wide, and just a hint of fear bloomed in them. But she nodded to show that she understood.

"And what do I do when I get there?" she asked.

"That, my girl," said the wizard, "is entirely up to you."

"Come with me," said Alma.

The old man looked at her in surprise. He started to answer, paused, then shook his head. "This is for you to do," he said softly. "Alone."

Balan placed his hand on his sister's shoulder and glared at Bellenmore.

"She must go alone," repeated the wizard.

*   *   *

THE GUARDIAN OF MEMORY

Grimwold paused and looked at the sky. "I'm taking too long to tell this. They're going to want me down below soon."

"You can't stop now!" cried Ivy. "What happened to Alma?"

"Well she came through, of course. But you know how that goes. You've done it yourself."

"But what *then*?"

Grimwold glanced at the sky again. "Then you and I went back down the cliff," he said abruptly. "Because it is not a good idea to keep the queen waiting."

Ivy started to protest again, but he raised his hand. "I have to tell the whole thing down there anyway," he reminded her. "You'll hear soon enough."

She sighed, and turned to follow him back down the path. When she did, she gasped in astonishment. The gathering of unicorns was complete. There must have been a thousand or more of them waiting in the grotto below. And though the sky was settling into darkness, from their gathered horns came a glow that lit the night, a glory that brought a sharp sting of tears to her eyes.

"They *are* beautiful," said the old dwarf. For a moment there was no hint of gruffness in his voice, only love and wonder.

Ivy nodded, unable to speak.

They made their way back down the trail, which was lit by the glory of unicorns, passing near enough to the waterfall on several turns that its spray dampened their clothes.

At the base of the cliff Cloudmane stood waiting for them.

"Let it be me," she said. "I want to be the next Guardian."

"You're mad," replied Grimwold, brushing past her.

Ivy hesitated. She knew she should follow Grimwold. But the unicorn, whom she had not met before, was clearly in great distress. She stopped, glanced uneasily at the dwarf, who did not look back to see if she was still coming, then put her hand on Cloudmane's neck. The mane felt like living silk.

"What is it?" she asked softly.

Cloudmane simply shook her head and turned away. Trotting silently back to join the others, she melted into the glory so smoothly that Ivy lost track of her in just seconds.

The girl sighed. Grimwold was far ahead of her now, and she scurried to catch up.

Before she had gone ten paces, a pair of tall stallions barred her path.

"Only Grimwold goes on from here," said one of them, gently but firmly. "The two-legs stand over there."

Ivy started to protest, then remembered it was a privilege to be here at all. She looked after Grimwold and realized that following him now would be like walking out onto a stage during a play—or rushing up to the pulpit during a church service. She turned in the direction the unicorn had indicated and saw a handful of humans and near-humans (including two elves and a gnome). They were standing beneath a clump of blue-green trees that were almost like the pine trees of home, but somehow different, too, of course. She recognized Master Chang, the painter, and old Madame Leonetti; the others were strangers to her.

She went to stand with the group.

The ceremony began.

The queen spoke first, greeting the gathered glory with what was clearly great joy. Yet there was sorrow in her voice as well.

Then came a song that was made not of sound but of light, and which Ivy heard not with her ears but with her heart.

When the song was over a tall stallion walked to the front of the group. He stood for a moment, then trumpeted a call that pierced the night, seeming to split the sky itself. A deep silence—a quiet unlike anything Ivy had ever experienced before—descended over the clearing. Even the waterfall seemed to have fallen silent.

The stallion spoke into that silence in a voice that was no more than a whisper, but that carried to the farthest edges of the glory. "We are here to choose the next Guardian of Memory. It is a position of honor and horror, of strength and sorrow, of glory and grief. He who fills it must be strong and swift, brave of heart and fleet of foot, able to endure not only pain and loss but the piercing joy of unexpected love that cannot last. To ready your hearts, listen once more to the story of the First Guardian."

Into the silence stepped Grimwold. The old dwarf began to speak, telling them all that he had told Ivy and more, adding details of the unicorns' first passage to Luster and how it had come to be.

Though Ivy had just heard the story, she hung on every word, drinking it in, trying to understand still more deeply. By the time Grimwold came to the point where he had left off before, she felt as if she were not hearing the story, but living it.

Now, when Alma had entered the land of the unicorns, she had—as should be no surprise—adventures strange and wondrous. She was captured by the delvers and held prisoner for three years. In her escape, she saved a young princeling named Windfoot, who was much beloved of his mother the queen. When the two arrived at the court, the grateful queen offered Alma a boon.

Alma stood, small and quiet. She looked around at the unicorns. Gathering her breath, and her courage, she said, "Come home."

A murmur of horror rippled through the glory.

"Come home," said Alma again, and this time there were tears coursing down her cheeks. "Something good is dying without you." She stepped toward the queen, and touched her, which was a great crime. But the queen did not move away.

Pressing her cheek to the queen's, burying her face in that mane that felt like spun cloud and smelled of the sea and the forest and something more, something that cannot be named, Alma whispered, "Hearts grow hard and weary. Pain spreads, and joy diminishes. Those who hated you hate you still, but those who loved you, or would have loved you, or wanted to love you but never had the chance are being scraped hollow by a loss they don't understand. Come home. Please come home. We are withering without you."

"The world is not kind to us, child," whispered the queen.

"It is even unkinder without you," replied Alma fiercely.

Then, her face pressed close to the queen's ear, the storyteller's daughter began to sing of all that the unicorns had left behind, the good and the bad, the oceans and the forest. She sang all that she had seen in her long wandering to find the unicorns. Pulsing through her song was the sorrow she herself had felt with their passing. Beneath that quivered the love of things unseen and mysteries unsolved—of untouched joy waiting just past the next moment—that had vanished with the passing of the unicorns.

As Alma sang, the queen remembered all the humans the unicorns had loved over the years, humans who had loved them back with open hearts, humans who had fought and died for them. She remembered, too, the world that had given them birth, a world no more beautiful than Luster, but no less so, either. And she thought of her own son, whom Alma had saved from the delvers, and finally she said, "Peace, girl. Be silent. Here is what I will grant you. From this time forth, there shall always be one unicorn—one and one alone—who lives in the world of our birth. That unicorn will have to be enough, enough to remind you of what was, and what can be. He will live alone, in the high places. He will not be seen often, or by many. But his presence should be enough to keep something alive in you. He will guard the memory of what has passed to this world, and the sight of him will help to keep it alive. Those who know such things will know, and those who understand such things will understand, and it will be, if not enough, then something. Something."

Then she turned to her son Windfoot and said, "Will you be the first?"

And Windfoot agreed, and so it was, and so it will be. Windfoot returned to the land of the humans for five and twenty years, and when his time was up a glory of unicorns gathered to choose a new Guardian of Memory, who went to take his place. And again it was done, and again, and yet again, for these many centuries, though not all the Guardians of Memory survived their full five and twenty years. For the hunting still goes on, and the world is full of danger.

And now the night for choosing is upon us once more, and that is the tale of its beginning.

His story finished, Grimwold came to stand beside Ivy.

A deep silence filled the grotto.

Into that silence came the voice of the queen, sighing across the glory like wind through clover. "Willing hero, willing victim, child of strength and pain, the chosen one must walk alone in paths of sorrow for the sake of those we have left behind. Who will step forward to try the wheel?"

Silently, about a hundred stallions moved to the front of the glory. Then, to Ivy's surprise, Madame Leonetti stepped forward, too. In her hands was a wreath made of white and yellow flowers that Ivy did not recognize. The old woman held the wreath to her side, at shoulder height. The first of the unicorns came forward, and took it with his horn. He held it for a moment, then—looking both disappointed and relieved—bent his head so that the next unicorn could take it from him.

In this way the wreath passed from one unicorn to another, with no decision being made.

"What are they waiting for?" asked Ivy. "How will they know?"

But Grimwold only shook his head and whispered, "Watch!"

From horn to horn went the wreath, without a sign of change, until only three volunteers remained. Though the queen appeared unworried, Grimwold was beginning to grow fretful.

When the last unicorn took the wreath, a cry of astonishment went up. The reason for the cry was not that something had happened, but that it *hadn't*.

No decision had been made. No new Guardian had been chosen.

The queen looked toward Madame Leonetti. "What

does it mean? Can the magic have failed after all these centuries?"

Madame Leonetti spread her hands. "I really don't—"

She was interrupted by an outburst from among the unicorns. "Let me try!" called Cloudmane, shouldering her way past a pair of stallions considerably taller than herself. "Let me try!"

"This is not for you," said one of the stallions gruffly. "Go back, Cloudmane."

"It's clearly not for you!" she replied defiantly. "None of you have been chosen. Will we let our old world wither, then? Shall we give up being Guardians because of your stubborn male pride? Will we leave Night Eyes stranded there forever? *Or will you let me try?*"

"Let her try," whispered the queen.

Madame Leonetti smiled, and extended the wreath.

Moving carefully, Cloudmane thrust her horn through its center.

For a moment the only sound was that of the waterfall. Then there was a crackle of power, and under it a murmur of astonishment from the gathered unicorns. The wreath began to vibrate. Light danced across its surface.

Madame Leonetti dropped her hold on the wreath and stepped back. Suspended in the air, Cloudmane's horn still at its center, the wreath began to spin. The light on its surface grew brighter, spiraling around the green leaves like mist made of fire. The crackle changed to a hum, the hum to a note like a bell. The wreath began to grow, and as it did, it became a window to the other world, the world the unicorns had fled; a window to Earth.

The view was that of a mountaintop.

At its peak stood Night Eyes, son of Manda Seafoam, who for twenty-five years had walked the hills of Earth, a Guardian of the ancient memory of unicorns, a silent, unseen reminder of lost joy and the possibility of healing. He looked toward them, but obviously could not see them, as if his attention had been drawn by the sound, but the door had not yet opened.

Then with a sudden flash of light, the door did open. The worlds linked. The homeward path was complete.

Trumpeting his joy, Night Eyes leaped forward, bounding through the circle of light to where the glory of unicorns stood waiting.

But no sooner through than he stopped in shock.

"Cloudmane!" he gasped. "*You* are the next Guardian?"

"Who else?" she asked softly.

"Quickly!" cried Madame Leonetti. "The magic will last but a moment longer."

"But why?" asked Night Eyes, his voice filled with sorrow. "Why, Cloudmane?"

Cloudmane lay her neck against his. "I need to know what you know, my beloved. Before I can be your full partner I must walk the hills of Earth, know its people, experience its beauty and its terror. Until I do, we cannot truly be together."

"But that does not explain how—"

"No time!" said Madame Leonetti, even more urgently than before. "The door will not stay open much
longer. You must go now, Cloudmane. *Now!*"

The opening was shimmering. With a cry, Cloudmane
leaped through the glowing circle, onto the mountaintop
where Night Eyes had stood but a moment earlier.

The circle closed with a rush and a snap.

The wreath fell to the ground, no longer green but a
brittle, burnt brown.

Earth was gone.

The door was gone.

Cloudmane was gone.

A song rose from the unicorns, a new version of the
prayer they always uttered for the Guardian of Memory.
"Guide her and guard her, Powers that Be. Love her and
watch over her on her journey. Bring her home safe
to us."

Soaring above all the other voices was that of Night
Eyes. On the very last word he differed in what he sang,
ending with a sob on, "Bring her home safe to *me*."

For a moment, all stood in silence. Then Night Eyes
bowed to the queen.

"I still don't understand," he said, his voice husky with
loss. "How can this be? I know why she wanted to go.
But how could it *happen?*"

The queen shook her head from side to side, the tip of
her horn inscribing an arc of light. "I do not know."

"I do," said Madame Leonetti. Her voice was frail, and

she had to work hard to be heard above the waterfall, which was sounding again. But the shape of the grotto brought her words to even the most distant ears.

"You have forgotten the nature of the magic. The exact wording of the spell as first created called for the Guardian of Memory to be 'the unicorn with the deepest love for those left behind.' Clearly, that was Cloudmane."

The queen shook her head. "Since the beginning of our connection, the deepest ties between human and unicorn have been between stallions and young maidens. How could Cloudmane have more love for those left behind?"

After a long silence Ivy said, "I think I know."

The queen turned to her. "Speak, child."

Ivy glanced around, trying to fight down a surge of panic. So many eyes were turned on her! Tangling her fingers in her long red hair, she gathered her courage. Finally she spoke.

"When Night Eyes went to be the Guardian, Cloudmane was left behind. That's why she can love those left behind on Earth. She knows what it's like to be left, because she's felt it herself."

"As have I," said Madame Leonetti, moving to place a hand on Night Eyes's shoulder.

"You were left behind?" he asked.

"Actually, I have both left someone behind and been left behind by him. His name was Balan, and he was my brother."

Ivy gasped. "You can't be—"

The old woman drew back her hood. Her face was lined with deep wrinkles, but in her eyes was something strong and wonderful. "Alma? Of course I am. With the blessings of the unicorns, one can live a long time in this place. Not, alas, without growing old. I left Balan behind when I came to Luster to beg the unicorns to return home, and left him even further behind when I chose to come back and live here. And now I have been left behind, too, because my brother is long dead, as are all the humans I knew when I was your age. It's been a rich life, child. But it is lonely. To leave. To be left. It's lonely, but it's what we do."

Ivy moved to stand beside the old woman. Alma Leonetti wrapped one arm around the girl's shoulder, the other around Night Eyes's neck. Together they looked toward the spark that still hung, flickering and fading, in the sky where Cloudmane had disappeared. A reminder of a reminder, it burned its way into their hearts, even as it vanished.

TEARING DOWN
THE UNICORNS

- JANNI LEE SIMNER -

K aren was tearing down the unicorns.

She pulled poster after poster from the wall above her bed, throwing them down to the floor beside her. A unicorn with pink ribbons in its mane and butterflies dancing around its horn ripped loudly away from the plaster. A unicorn flying through a green field, a wreath of wildflowers about its neck, tore in half as she pulled. Bits of paper and brittle tape were everywhere— on Karen's frilly bedspread, on our pink carpet, on my own bed and dresser, halfway across the room.

I stood in the doorway, too startled at first to do anything but watch. Some of those posters had been up for years, for longer than I could remember. Karen reached for another poster, this one of a unicorn with gentle purple eyes curled beside a rabbit in a snow-covered field.

"Stop it!" I yelled. Karen spun around, noticing me for

the first time, looking more than a little annoyed at being interrupted.

"What are you *doing*?" I asked, a little more quietly—but not much.

Karen rolled her eyes. I knew she wished I'd just go away. She'd been like that ever since she'd started junior high. Until then we'd done everything together, so much so that people called me "Karen's shadow." Mostly I didn't mind, though sometimes I wished they would use my name, Stacey, instead. But lately Karen didn't seem to have the time to be bothered by either a shadow or a sister two years younger than her.

"What does it look like I'm doing?" she asked, her voice dripping sarcasm.

"Okay then, *why* are you doing it?" I stepped into the room and stood beside her.

Karen sighed dramatically—she'd been doing that a lot lately, too—and said, "Just look at them, Stacey." On her wall only a couple of posters were left. One was a copy of some flat-looking medieval tapestry, a unicorn sitting quietly inside a low fence. The other was of a girl on a silvery unicorn's back, both its mane and her pale hair flowing softly out behind them. Sometimes I wished I could find a unicorn of my own like that, even though I wasn't so sure unicorns were real in the first place.

I'd only admitted to Karen about not being sure once, back when we were both younger. Karen's eyes had turned steely and cold. "Of course they're real," she'd said. "Assuming you believe hard enough." Her voice had made it clear that *she* believed, so I bit my lip, did my best to believe as well, and didn't ask her again.

Yet now Karen was the one who looked at the posters on her wall, on her floor, and repeated, "Just look at them. They're so sappy, so stupid, so—" She hesitated, searching for the right word. "So fake." She yanked down the last two posters. Then she snatched the whole pile up from the floor, as if ready throw them all away. My stomach knotted painfully at the thought.

"No!" I ran over and grabbed the unicorns away from her. More tape and paper fluttered to the floor around us. I clutched the posters tightly to my chest, knowing I was crinkling them but not willing to let go.

Karen just stared at me. "What's your problem, Stacey?"

I stared back. "How can you just throw them out?" Karen had spent years collecting those unicorns. I'd helped, looking through racks of posters with her whenever we went to the drugstore or mall.

"What do you care?" Karen gestured toward her now-bare wall, pink paint scarred white where the tape had been. "It's not like you ever believed in unicorns anyway, even back when I did."

The first part of her sentence bugged me—I'd tried to believe, after all, tried to be as much like Karen as I could —but the second part was worse.

Even back when I did. Karen didn't believe, either, not anymore. I don't know why that bothered me much more than what I did or didn't believe, but it did. I took the posters and dumped them on my own bed, on top of my pillow.

Karen shook her head. "What are you going to do? Hang them on *your* walls?"

"Maybe."

Karen shrugged, as if she suddenly didn't care what I did or didn't do. She grabbed a jacket off her dresser and started for the door.

"Where are you going?" Without thinking, I started across the room to follow her.

"Out with my friends." She draped the jacket over her shoulders and glanced back at me. "Alone." She whirled away and left without saying anything more. I listened as her footsteps crossed the house and the front door slammed behind her.

How come every time Karen said she wanted to be alone, I was the one who wound up feeling lonely?

I flopped down at the foot of my bed and stared at the posters beside me. A serious-looking unicorn, standing beside a pale green-and-pink castle, stared back at me.

I didn't have as much wall space as Karen, thanks to the window above my bed, and some of the space I did have was already filled with pictures of Karen, Dad, and me. Still, I got up, and I began taping posters to my wall. The unicorns were crumpled from being pulled down and then grabbed; those that had been torn apart wouldn't fit together again quite right. The tape on one unicorn pulled loose, and it fluttered back down to the bed.

I sighed and looked out the window. Our room faces

out onto the woods, or at least as much of the woods as you get in the suburbs. Dad told me once that our yard is almost an acre, and I know by the way he said it that that's supposed to be a lot. We have a small patio near the house, but most of the yard is filled with tall oaks and maples, hiding the chain-link fence beyond them.

Karen and I used to play out back a lot, Karen insisting that our house bordered some enchanted forest, leading us back and forth among the trees, never taking the same route twice.

As I looked out now, I saw bright red and yellow leaves clinging to the branches. Browner leaves lay on the ground, among the weeds Dad was always bugging us to help him pull up. I opened the window a crack, letting in the crisp smell of autumn. A single leaf trembled free and drifted, very slowly, to the ground.

Did something else move among those trees? I saw another branch tremble, caught a glimpse of autumn gold —but then I saw only leaves and trees once more.

Karen didn't come back home until just before dinner. After dinner, she stayed in the living room with Dad, doing her homework. I never had as much homework as Karen, and I'd already finished it all, so I hung around for a while, then went back to our room.

Another poster had fallen down, and those still on my wall looked more ragged and messy than ever. I knelt on the bed and started retaping them. Outside, the night was surprisingly clear, full of glittering stars. My breath frosted faintly against the window. The trees were shadows beneath a moonless sky.

A sudden movement caught my eye. I dropped the poster in my hand and strained for a better look. I saw a flash of something brighter than autumn leaves, brighter than the flames in our fireplace last winter.

The light faded, leaving the yard darker than before. The glow from the houses around ours seemed suddenly very far away. Then the darkness faded, too, and at last I saw the creature that stood only a few yards away from my window, right at the patio's edge.

Its body was the color of burning gold, a deep, hot color I don't really know how to describe. The air all around it glowed with gold light. Its mane blew restlessly about, like flames flickering in some wind. Its eyes, staring straight at me, shone red as embers. And on its forehead—

On its forehead was a single horn, bright as fire, so bright my eyes hurt just from looking at it. I didn't look away, though.

It was like no poster I'd ever seen. But Karen had been right, before she'd torn her posters down. Unicorns were real. And this one was more stunning than I'd ever imagined.

More than anything, I wanted to be outside with it.

I almost told Karen first. She was still in the living room, arguing with Dad about some boy at school. But even as I thought about her, the unicorn pawed restlessly at the patio. I feared if I left the room, even for a moment, it would be gone when I returned.

Besides, after the way she'd pulled her posters down, I wasn't so sure Karen deserved to see a real unicorn now.

I opened my window. Chilly air flooded the room, along with the faint smell of burning ash. Our house was only one story; Karen and I had both snuck out the window before, at different times when Dad wouldn't let us outside. When I was smaller, I'd needed Karen to help pull me back up inside afterward. That was a long time ago, though. Now I lifted out the window screen, climbed over the sill, and jumped easily to the ground.

The unicorn still stood at the edge of the patio, watching me through smoldering red eyes. I heard its deep breathing, saw its breath come out in puffs of white frost —or maybe smoke; I couldn't tell. Very slowly, I walked toward it. The air grew warm as I approached, then hot, nothing like autumn was supposed to feel. Finally I stood right in front of the unicorn, bathed in heat so strong it reminded me of the fire Dad had built when we'd gone camping last summer. Hot gold light reflected off my bare arms; sweat trickled down my neck. The smell of ash was much stronger than before.

For a long moment I just stood there, staring, still not quite able to believe in spite of all I saw. Then I reached out to touch the unicorn's golden mane.

My hand brushed burning fire. I gasped and pulled away. The unicorn threw back its head and let out a deep, throaty yell, like the roar of flames on dry wood. I stumbled backward. My palm began to throb, pain much sharper than the time I'd touched the burner of our stove.

I clenched my hand into a fist and shook it, but the pain wouldn't go away.

The unicorn kicked up its hooves; when they hit the ground again, sparks flew up from the patio. It turned from me and ran into the trees.

I expected it to run away, to jump the fence and never return. But before it got that far it whirled and raced back toward me. Halfway to me it whirled away once more, running wildly through the trees. Flickers of flame trailed behind it, leaving gold sparks in the air where it passed. Dry leaves crackled beneath its feet. My palm still burned; any moment I expected the leaves to catch fire and burn, too. My heart pounded hard in my chest.

Yet I kept watching. The unicorn was the wildest, most frightening thing I'd ever seen—but also the most beautiful. Soon I realized there was a pattern to its running, one that kept it from ever taking the same path twice. It wasn't just running. It was dancing, a fiery dance like nothing I'd ever seen before.

The burning in my hand spread through the rest of my body, dulling to a smoldering ache as it did. Something about that ache urged me forward. I wanted, more than anything, to follow, to dance with the unicorn.

I watched it a few seconds more, memorizing its pattern, learning the steps of its dance.

Then I took a deep breath and ran after it.

As I drew close the unicorn spun to face me, blocking my path, casting gold light on the trees and grass and weeds all around us. I skidded to a halt. Heat made my shirt stick to my skin, like the middle of a sweltering summer day. The unicorn snorted, and its steamy breath stung my cheek. It whirled away and continued running.

I ran after it again, but again it turned to stop me. I took a step forward, but the unicorn didn't move. It didn't want me to join its dance.

Tears stung at the corners of my eyes; I fiercely brushed them away. The smoldering heat inside me turned up a notch. With that heat came anger, fiercer than the ordinary anger I sometimes felt around Dad or Karen or the kids at school. Why should I have to keep from dancing just because someone—even a unicorn—told me not to?

If the unicorn wouldn't let me dance with it, I decided, I'd just have to dance on my own.

I looked at the sky. A huge, nearly full moon had risen over the trees. For a moment I stared at it, not sure how to begin. Then I chose a direction, and I ran.

At first I felt kind of silly, running every which way with no real purpose. But then I began to find patterns of my own, directions in which I wanted to go. I ran faster. Leaves crunched beneath my feet, and I kicked them up all around me. Wind brushed my cheek, threw my hair into my face. Trees flew by, flashes of red and yellow, sometimes lit by the unicorn's light, sometimes not.

The hot embers within me turned to a dancing fire, urging me on, so fast I felt as if I were flying. I laughed aloud, and the sound was like timber catching flame. I looked around for the unicorn, wanting to show it that I could dance just fine without it, that I could run as fast as I wanted.

The unicorn stood at the edge of the patio, watching me. I stopped short and stared back, meeting its fiery eyes with my own.

For several heartbeats neither of us moved. The moon inched higher in the sky, turning from yellow to silver-white. Then the unicorn nodded, a gesture surprisingly serious and respectful. I had the sudden strange feeling that it approved of my running, that it had wanted me to run all along. But if that was true, why had it gotten in my way?

Without warning, the unicorn reared back and roared again. Leaves rustled wildly around us. The unicorn's horn flared, so bright I had to shut my eyes. Against closed eyelids I felt a searing flash of light and heat.

The heat faded, leaving the night cool once more. When I opened my eyes, I stood alone in the yard. The air was heavy with the chill scent of autumn — and, more faintly, the memory of fire and ash.

"Stacey?" The voice was Karen's, calling from the bedroom. I started slowly toward the window, not sure I was ready to talk with—or be with—anyone else yet. It was the first time I could ever remember wanting to be alone.

Maybe for some things you had to be alone. Like to run as fast as you could, or to dance with burning fire.

Maybe being alone was the only way you could see a unicorn.

"What are you doing out there?" Karen looked down

at me as if I were crazy, as if she hadn't climbed out the window plenty of times herself, as recently as last summer. "Couldn't you just use the door, like normal people?"

I didn't answer; instead I reached over the windowsill to climb back inside. I braced a foot against the house, but slipped as I tried to scramble up. I must have been more tired than I'd thought from all that running. Karen reached out and helped pull me in, as if I were still a little kid.

"What happened to your hand?" she asked. I glanced down. A bright red welt crossed my palm where the unicorn's mane had burned me.

"Are you all right?" Karen sounded almost worried.

I shrugged. "What do you care?" Karen had made it clear she didn't want anything to do with me, after all.

Karen looked puzzled. "Of course I care. You're my sister."

"Then why don't you want to do stuff together anymore?"

Suddenly Karen seemed uncomfortable. "Caring and wanting to be together all the time aren't the same thing, you know?" She stared at me, as if that should have made perfect sense. "Sometimes a person gets tired of having a shadow."

I thought of the unicorn, not letting me follow, but not minding, even approving, of my running on my own. All of a sudden Karen's words did make sense, at least a little. All of a sudden, I wasn't so sure I wanted to be her shadow, anyway.

Karen's posters were still around us, a few of them on my wall, most of them on my bed. Quiet silvery unicorns stared at us through gentle eyes, birds and butterflies and rainbows dancing all around them.

No, I thought, those weren't unicorns. The golden, fiery creature outside had been a unicorn. Unicorns weren't gentle or tame. Where had I, or Karen, or anyone else ever gotten the idea that they were?

"You can have your posters back," I said.

Karen just shook her head. "I already told you I don't want them. They're so fake."

"I know they are. But they're still your posters, not mine." They always had been, for all that I'd helped Karen choose them, for all that I'd tried to believe in them just because she did.

I glanced out the window. The moon was high now, the autumn leaves bright beneath it—though not as bright as they'd been by the unicorn's light. I touched my palm; the skin was cool. The unicorn's fire wasn't in my hand anymore. It still burned, though, somewhere deeper inside me.

I grinned at Karen. Then I reached for the posters above my bed.

And I started tearing them down.

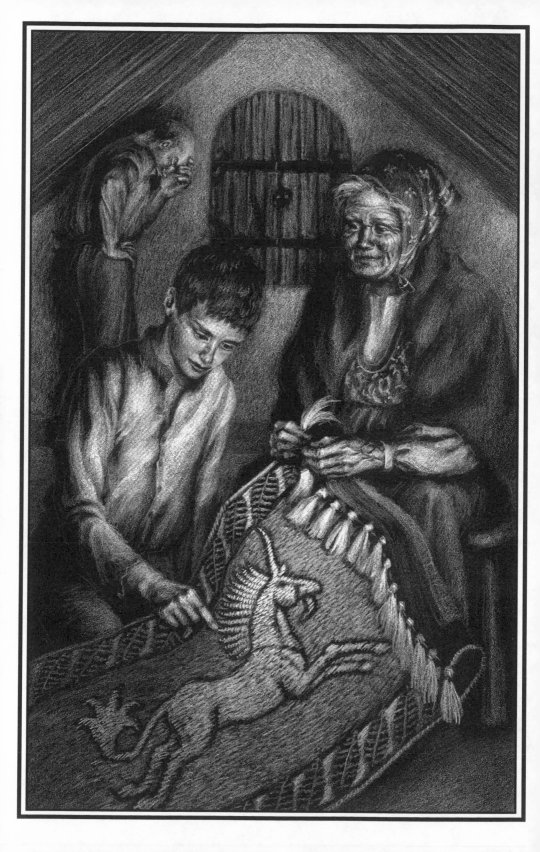

BEYOND THE FRINGE

– GREGORY MAGUIRE –

Boots thundered on the cobbles outside, and Gram drew her shawl around her. She raised her voice as if to drown out the sound of the midnight threat. "He lived in the high places," she went on, "places of wind and light. Theaters of stone and air. He stood on cliffs and watched clouds below him build and tumble." Her hands, gnarled and spry, worked as she spoke. They pulled, stretched, laced, tied, knotted. The thread was narrow but strong; its escaping hairs gave off a white nimbus, like dandelion fluff.

"But Gram, did you ever *see* a unicorn?" said Cor.

"Hush with this nonsense!" said Ox, seething, but he did not look at his mother-in-law or his son. Ox might as well have been addressing the army of the night, at its work of smashing windows, thudding on the barricaded doors with a battering ram. The fifth night in a row of terrorizing by brigands masked, mute, and merciless. On the other nights the raids had been brief, as if the invaders had suspected a quick reprisal. Tonight their confidence was strong, and the commotion less scattershot.

Cor and Gram exchanged glances.

"Did you ever see a unicorn, Gram?" asked the boy in a softer voice.

"I did," she said. In the shadowy attic, lit only by the stub of a candle, her face could still look like a clutch of daffodils glowing in sunlight. "On the western slope of High Thistledown. Above the treeline. He was stopped on an outcrop of mossy rock, pawing as if cleaning soil from his hoofs. His head was bowed, and the horn—oh, Cor!—your heart would leap to see it! It wasn't the perfect spiral peg that woodturners fashion on their lathes. Nor was it the crystal ice that glassblowers like to encourage from their pipes. It was—" Her voice faltered.

Cor dropped his gaze to the carpet that Gram was finishing with fringe. The carpet was draped across her knees and spread out at her feet. "It was just like this," he said. He knelt forward and touched the ivory-colored silhouette of the unicorn, knotted into the warp and weft. "His horn curved upward a little."

"And was bone, not glass," said Gram.

"You're betraying your grandson," said Ox suddenly. "With your airy tales of magical beasts! For shame, for shame! And the brutes down there doing their best to level us! To make us rubble, and rot, and ruin! How can you feed the boy such faërie tripe!"

"Ox," said Gram, "we are hidden in an attic, waiting in

the gloom for our allies in the next valley to rescue us. They do not come and they do not come. Every night for five nights they do not come, though by day we have lit the beacons to send the dark smoke messages aloft, saying COME, COME. Maybe our neighbors have joined the enemy, and in strange disguises are looting below. Or maybe our neighbors have been rooted out as we are being rooted out. Either way, there is no harm in envisioning the unicorn in this dark hour."

"There is no good in it," said Ox, but his mother-in-law only smiled at him with tired eyes and said gently, "The forces of the Storm King have not yet torched your house, dear Ox, but they have laid waste your heart. Cor is only a boy in this hard time. Let me busy him with visions."

"Lies," said Ox, but more softly.

"Memories," said Gram, more tartly.

Cor did not like to see his father and his grandmother argue. He rolled onto the carpet and flipped the finished edge over himself like a blanket. The newly added fringe fell in fingertip softness against his cheeks and lips; he closed his eyes. A feeling something like the beginning of a sneeze, but deeper in his chest, began to roil. It was love, or fear, or regret; he did not know how to identify it, and he didn't care. What was important was that it was a real feeling; it was here and now.

When it happened, the sense of the *here* and *now* was important to Cor. Mostly because it was so often missing, squeezed out between the memory of a happy past that had come to an end, and the hopes for a happy future that could never be. Three years ago, Cor's mother had been the victim of one of the early attacks by the unknown rabble-rousers. Her corpse had been found on the hillside, left in a pile of similarly slaughtered sheep that she'd been tending. Ox had hidden Cor's eyes and not let him look. But in that one awful day Cor had gone from being a ten-year-old boy to a ten-year-old man.

On that same awful day Ox had gone from being a husband to a widower. Within weeks, his fine thick hair had thinned and fallen out; his shoulders stooped, his eyes dulled. Gram had given up her own small cottage at the other end of the tiny village to come tend to their needs. "The boy has to have someone, something," she said to her son-in-law. "We all need each other now. The times are hard, and will get harder, Ox." With her, she brought three iron pots, a chest of dark skirts and shawls, some sacks of wool for carding, spinning, weaving; a spindle, a shuttle, and a loom. For the first four months after the murder, the song of Gram's spinning wheel was the only music in Ox's household.

Cor had stumbled about in a daze. The village children avoided him, as if his mother had somehow brought her own odd doom upon herself. Yet by the time a year had passed, there had been a series of attacks. It became clear that the murder of Cor's mother was not random violence by a madman but the beginning of the Storm King's careful campaign of terrorism, though for what purposes none could guess. But by now the village children had grown accustomed to shunning Cor, and he had grown accustomed to being more or less alone.

The here and the now of his body's warmth, wrapped in the carpet, was rich fare indeed, but the here and the now also included what was painful. He threw the edge of the carpet back. His father was kneeling in the shadows, looking down through the unpainted shutters. Ox had not shaved in five days; his chin and cheeks were rough as the underside of the carpet. He bent forward as he peered between the slats of the broad attic window shutters. "They are at Fellamy's cottage," he said. "Please, may she be hidden!"

"She is hidden," said Gram stoutly.

"You know? How do you know?" he said, turning to her. "Your old crippled legs don't let you up and down the stairs anymore! Who have you been gossiping with when we're out foraging for food in the dawn wind?"

"I know she's hidden," said Gram, "because I know Fellamy, and I know she would be hidden. She's no fool. Don't ask me where, for I don't know."

"They've touched a torch to the thatch on her goat shed," said Ox.

"Of the goats, I cannot vouch," said Gram, and sure enough, there was the distant scream of goats wretched with fear. Gram bent over her work; her fingers seemed to stumble at the sound. "I will hurry and finish this at least," she murmured.

"Your wools and yarns and pretty work will burn," said Ox. "Why are we not out there fighting?" He punched his fist against a wooden post, and then popped his hand in his armpit and cursed beautifully.

"I saw the unicorn run," said Gram to Cor. "It was not the heavy gallump-gallump of a pony, nor the hungry lollop of a dog, nor the sideswiping streak of a cat. It was more like a flag in the wind. Or like a wave curling its fingers as it does, fifty yards off the strand, ready to crash into pebbles of light and foam."

"Did he run away from you?" said Cor.

"He ran toward me," said Gram.

"Good mercy," said Ox in his most courteous voice, "can you please not fill up the boy's ears like this? With all that we hold dear being ripped from us, and we so powerless to prevent it?"

"We will not have our *beliefs* ripped from us," said Gram. She tugged so hard that she broke her knot, and had to begin it again. "Ox, you always had to work too hard on this hardscrabble mountain to go exploring its high passes for the holy sights! You did the job of a good husband and a good father, but you cannot deny me what I have seen with my own eyes!"

"And when were you last gamboling on High Thistledown?" hissed Ox.

"It was not recently, to be sure," she said. "Cor, hold the end of this last hank of fringe while I cut it to length. No," she continued, "these arthritic hips don't let me up and down the stairs, as you say. This was some time ago —maybe even before you were born, Ox. I don't remember the year exactly."

"What were you doing on High Thistledown?" said Ox.

"If you must know," she said, "I was newly betrothed, and my fiancé and I were out taking the air." She looked defiantly at Ox. "Your father-in-law had less clouded eyes than you."

Cor looked up in amazement. Gram was so stout, so fretted with wrinkles at every joint, so short of breath even when sitting down! It was hard to imagine that she had a past, a past even further back than Cor's own. It was hard to imagine a past for Gram that included walking with a young man who loved her, out under the canopy of wind, on the carpet of flower-strewn grass!

"So the unicorn came trotting along to me," she said. "I was walking ahead of my betrothed, having run from him in a game. I had a pair of scissors in my apron pocket, for I meant to cut some of the blue ferns that grow only on the highest peak, and brew some blue fern tea when I returned."

"Why?" said Cor.

"Blue fern tea is good for the bride-to-be," said Gram. "Clarifies the dreams and shows the future. Remember that, Cor, if you want to marry."

"Oh, that he would live that long to make such a choice!" said Ox in a low voice, and he sunk his head into his hands and wept.

Cor wanted to comfort his father. But he didn't know how. The man was unhinged with the hopelessness of their plight. "Come," said Cor, in a voice boys don't often use with their fathers. "Come, get yourself warm in this carpet. Come, we can share it." He lifted the finished edge while Gram continued to knot the fringe on the final six inches of the other end. "It's very warm and you will feel better."

Ox did not answer and did not look up, but his crying stopped.

"The unicorn came running up to me," said Gram, in a lower voice. She did not care to agitate her son-in-law. "I was both honored and terrified. I sank to my knees, and the unicorn came to a kind of bow before me, and he lowered his horn into my aproned lap."

"Did you touch him?"

"I stroked his noble head," said Gram. "I bent over the unicorn's horn and scratched his ears. He looked at me as a good farm horse will, with one eye. His eye was blue, and it bulged somewhat. And what do you know: reflected in the slightly curved surface of the eye was I, and the high fields and cliffsides beyond, and even my betrothed coming gently up behind, slowing down, waiting, not to disturb us. It was as if all the world, everything I could ever love or need, was reflected in the unicorn's eye."

"Did he speak?"

"I don't believe they speak," said Gram, "or if they do, not to me."

"Did he sing? I thought they sang."

"Perhaps he hummed a little bit, or made a sound like purring," said Gram. "I can't remember that, but he might have."

The sounds of the goats outside had stopped. Either the goats had broken through their pens, driven wild by fear, or the burning thatch had collapsed upon them all.

"What then?" said Cor.

"What then," said Ox, a little mockingly, going back to the window, "or should I say, what now? I can hear little, and see nothing. Have they left us alone at last? One more day to live, waiting for one more night? If not our turn tonight, then when? How long can we last here?"

"The unicorn bent his head and nuzzled it into my lap," said Gram. "His mane was thick and silver, like a brush of silken bristles. It grew in a stripe some five inches wide, running from his forehead down his neck. I felt it with my hand. It was rich with possibility."

"And us with no possibility," said Ox. "Have you no charity, woman? As we're stuck here, holed up in an attic room, in an isolated village with no hope of escape by day or night—the only valley pass guarded by masked brigands, and the hillsides on either side shorn treeless by grazing sheep, affording no cover for us to hide behind! Rich with possibility! Are you mocking our plight? Have you become so old that you do not see what is happening?"

"I am still your elder," said Gram in a sharp voice, "and I intend to finish my story, Ox, so if you don't care to hear it, go outside and give yourself up to the secret servants of the Storm King if you must! Let me do my *work*!"

In a low voice, Ox said, "Forgive me, Gram."

She drew in a breath and started on the last set of knots. She motioned to Cor to hold the edge of the carpet steady on her lap, for now that she was at the last corner it had a tendency to slide to the floor. "I ruffled his feathery mane, and I looked in his eye," said Gram, "and the eye blinked, and I looked in it again. It seemed I was looking in it for a very long time. But later, my betrothed could say no more surely than I whether I looked for a minute or a month. I only know that the time came that I looked away again."

Cor nodded.

"Then I took my scissors," said Gram, "for I felt that the unicorn's eye had shown me what I needed to do. And I cut the mane off the unicorn, from brow to spine. It came in sprays, and gave off the most wonderful redolent odor of earth and sea and sunrise—I can't describe it. It was a bouquet of white grass, throbbing with life, and I gathered it up in my apron. When I was done, the unicorn blinked again, and his eye was misty; I couldn't see a reflection any longer. He struggled to his feet—the only movement I ever saw him make that wasn't graceful— and backed away, almost as if ashamed of what he had done. Then he turned and cantered up the field, toward the highest crest of the hill, and he disappeared on the other side."

"Oh," said Cor. He had wanted Gram to go for a ride somehow.

"Perhaps he was the last one," said Gram. "As far as I know, no one has ever seen a unicorn since."

"Certainly no one in my generation," said Ox. "Woman, am I to apologize for being rude?"

"You are to take care of yourself and your boy," said Gram. "What means rudeness to me, at my age?"

Ox's moment of softness was past; the bells in the church tower began to ring. "Is it all over?" he said. "Is someone announcing the arrival of help?"

"I believe," said Gram, no change of tone, "that it is the invaders announcing to any of us who remain hidden and hopeful that the last hope of help is gone. For the bells at night would bring our neighbors in the next village, certainly, if smoke by day did not. The invaders are saying that there are no more neighbors. They must be confident that they have killed the largest portion of our men of fighting age. They are taunting those who remain."

"Oh, Gram," said Cor, "but what happened to the mane that you cut?"

"Hush, you must listen to your father," said Gram, "for my story is done. Believe it or not, as you like, but the day will come when I will not be near you to tell you stories. Still, the eyes that look on you with love, dear boy, once looked into the eyes of a unicorn."

Cor couldn't bring himself to look his grandmother in the eyes at first. He felt shy in front of her, for the first time in his life.

Gram finished the last bit of fringe and said, "Now put the carpet out flat, and let us see how well the fringe lies. What a long effort this has been."

The carpet ran five feet long and two and a half feet wide. In the center was the image of a unicorn, capering, each of his legs strutting proudly, his mane ruffled like an open fan, his feathery tail displayed like the gush of a fountain. The body of the unicorn was cream colored, and the field of color against which he pranced was midnight blue, bordered with blue ferns. The fringe, five inches long, fell in a full wave on either end of the carpet.

"Enough room for you and your father," said Gram, satisfied. "If the day comes when you don't have this house, you can sleep on this carpet."

"It's beautiful, Gram," said Cor. "But tell me, what—"

"The bells have stopped—" said Ox. "Maybe—"

A sound from below. Sounds. The thud of an ax, the shriek of wood splintering. "Oh," said Ox, "oh!" There was no place to go; the shuttered window gave out on the alley, but it was too high up to jump. Ox grabbed a hunting knife, and said, "*Cor*! Hold the club as I showed you, and swing high, when you have to, with all the strength you have!"

"That's not the way," said Gram. "Open the window, Cor." Her voice was low and calm, but urgent; Cor obeyed. The two shutters pulled inward, and the casements swung outward. "Quick," said Gram, "quick now, Ox; it's time."

"Gram, say your prayers," said Ox, and gave his mother-in-law a hurried kiss, then whirled around to face the door.

"On the carpet, don't you see?" said Gram. "It's

ready!" She tried to pull herself from her bench, but she couldn't get a good handhold. "Cor! The carpet!"

Cor grabbed the end of it. "What?"

"Get on it!" she said. "Ox, it's ready! It's time to go!"

Ox didn't hear. He had the knife out. But Cor suddenly understood. "Come on, Gram," he cried, dragging at her arms. But she resisted, saying, "Not for me, there's not room enough. And I've had my day! There's room for two! Didn't I make it for you? Go on!"

Boots sounded on the stairs; men cried out at the hope for more victims. From behind, Cor threw his arms around his father and pulled. Ox fell backward onto the carpet and knocked the breath out of Cor. So for a moment the boy couldn't speak, he couldn't even say *thanks*, as the carpet began to tremble, like a beached canoe being played with by the rising tide. The carpet lifted, and Ox bellowed, "Gram!" But as the door opened, and the masked brigands plowed into the shadowy attic room, the carpet moved with grace and steadiness out the window.

Gram heard Cor cry, "Oh, Gram!" She raised her hand and blessed them both, and then turned to face the villains. Outside, the light from the burning church tower spilled through the fringe of the carpet, which glowed white as a unicorn's mane.

STEALING DREAMS

~ RUTH O'NEILL ~

When Michael Evans was a baby, his parents covered his room in magic wallpaper. They didn't realize this, of course; all they meant to do was decorate the walls with pleasant scenes of trees and birds and animals. Michael himself only discovered it when he was four, one night at bedtime.

As he was nearly ready to drift off to sleep, a rabbit hopped onto his bed from behind one of the trees on the wallpaper. It sat in a beam of moonlight, scrubbing its face with one paw. Michael moved to sit up, but the rabbit jumped back into the wallpaper and disappeared.

Michael began to watch the wallpaper whenever he could. At first, he saw nothing special, but day by day he became more and more aware of things moving in the background, until he had no trouble seeing activity wherever he looked. Birds built nests in the trees, hatched their eggs, taught their little ones to fly, all somehow inside the wallpaper. Deer bounded gracefully through fields or slept curled safely in hidden glades. Now and then a tortoise waddled by.

When Michael was six and came down with chicken pox, he hardly minded staying in bed all day, with so much to watch. He grew used to his magic wallpaper, but never told anyone else about it. It was his great secret, and it comforted him through the bad times when his parents started to fight, and when they got divorced and his father moved away. He also spent a great deal of time reading books to find out more about all the creatures he had found in his wallpaper. He learned about badgers and owls, porcupines and hawks. That was when he was eight.

By the time Michael was eleven, though, the wallpaper had begun to fade, and the magic seemed to be fading, too. First days, then weeks, then months went by when the wallpaper showed him nothing, no matter how hopefully he looked. Eventually, hope changed to frustration and mourning as he forced himself to admit that it seemed to have stopped altogether. So when his mother suggested that it was time for a change, he didn't complain. (Besides, his friend Patrick had recently teased him about his "baby room" in front of Carol Johnson and, worse still, Emily Tanner.)

Michael and his mother went shopping together, and Michael picked out a huge mural of a coral-reef scene. "We'll put it up this weekend," his mother told him.

That night, while the rolls of wallpaper that would make up the mural sat waiting in the corner of his room,

Michael saw the unicorn. It hadn't always been there, he was sure. It must have wandered in from some far-off place beyond the edges of his bedroom walls, a last flicker of the old magic. It strode confidently through the forest, its long white mane flowing back over the strong, white body. The small beard was shaggy yet somehow seemed well groomed. The horn looked like crystal, clear as the water in the forest pools the unicorn drank from. In contrast to the rest were the cloven hooves and large, soft eyes, both deeply black.

Nothing except the one rabbit had ever actually come out of the wallpaper, but Michael hoped he might be able to coax the unicorn into his room. Horses liked sugar, or so he had read; he decided to try that.

Quietly, Michael slid out of his bed and crept down the hall to the kitchen, where he took three cubes from the sugar bowl. He tiptoed back past his mother working at her computer. She didn't look up when he passed either way, but Michael was not quiet enough for a unicorn's ears. As he reentered his room, the unicorn was watching him.

A little nervously, Michael held out his hand to show the sugar cubes, then set them carefully on his dresser. He backed away from them, almost to the bedroom door again. The unicorn looked at the sugar, then at Michael, then back at the sugar. It tossed its head, seemed to consider a moment, and stepped out of the wallpaper into the room. Five delicate steps carried the unicorn to the dresser; it picked up the sugar with its lips, drew the cubes into its mouth, and crunched them down.

Finished, the graceful creature took a few steps toward Michael, stretching its head forward, sniffing. Michael reached out as far as he could without moving his feet, until his fingertips just brushed the tip of the crystal horn. A jolt of power tingled up his arm, and he jerked his hand back. The unicorn wheeled away from this sudden movement, running into the wallpaper and out of sight through the trees.

That night, when he finally managed to fall asleep, Michael had some amazing dreams: He went white-water rafting, then on a ballooning trip, and just before waking, on a scuba-diving adventure off a glorious coral reef like the one in the new mural they were going to put up. All of these were more vivid, more real than any dream he had had before, and he could remember them perfectly in every detail.

The next day, Michael tried to think of ways to keep the unicorn from disappearing when the old wallpaper came down. Leaving it up was one possibility, but he didn't think his mother would go along with that, with the new mural already paid for. The unicorn would have to stay on this side of the wall.

At school that day, he spent some extra time in the library, reading about unicorns. He was fascinated to learn that the word for the crystal horn he had touched was *alicorn*, and, more importantly, that a golden bridle could be used to capture a unicorn. But where to find one?

Michael wondered about golden bridles on and off all day. That night, though, he forgot about them as he brought the unicorn more sugar, and again touched the horn and felt the shock of magic at work. He could hardly wait to fall asleep, so of course it took longer, but when he did, the dreams were just as powerful as before. He went to sea to watch whales, and on an African safari as a world-famous photographer.

The next afternoon, Michael walked home deep in thought, wondering how to make a bridle out of gold, assuming he could get any. His mother's voice shook him out of his reverie as soon as he opened the door to the house, but her words didn't sink in.

"What, Mom?" he shouted down the hall.

She poked her head out of the office. "I said, there's a package for you on the table, a present from your father. I know your birthday isn't until next week, but you can open it now. He called, and says to watch the tape first."

Michael tore open the package and found a videotape tucked next to a very small wrapped present. He took them both into the living room, slid the tape into the VCR, and settled down on the couch with the remote.

When he turned on the TV and pressed the play button, his father appeared on the screen. "Hello, Michael," he said. He paused a moment, obviously leaving a space for Michael to say "hello" back, but Michael didn't say anything.

"Well, Michael, I'm sorry I didn't have enough money to fly out and visit you in person, but I borrowed a friend's video camera so you could at least see me. I didn't have much money for a present, either, so I'm giving you something of mine, something I've had since I was your age. It was your grandfather's before that. You can open your present now."

Michael stopped the tape and tore open the little package. Inside was a small piece of wood, about the size of a jackknife. It fit his hand comfortably, feeling smooth and well worn. A hard black square stuck out from one side of it. Michael looked at it curiously, then restarted the tape.

His father smiled out at him again. "Got it? Good. It's called a flint and steel, and it's an old way of lighting fires. Look at the black stone on the side." Michael nodded. "That's the flint. Now, look in the end. Pull out the small metal blade. That's the steel. You use it to scrape a bit of tinder off some wood. Then strike the steel against the flint to make sparks. There's even a secret compartment for storing a little tinder. Watch." In the video, Michael's father started a small fire, using only the flint and steel to ignite it. Michael copied the way he made the sparks; it took several tries, but he was thrilled when he made it work. He felt for the tinder compartment and pushed it open.

When he looked up at the television again, his father was looking quietly into the camera. After a few moments, he said, "Happy Birthday, Michael," and reached forward to stop the recording. Just before the picture cut out, a ray of sun glinted like gold off his hair.

Michael rewound the tape a few seconds and watched again, then touched his own hair thoughtfully. It was blond, just like his father's. The rest of the tape was forgotten as Michael ran down the hall to his room and closed the door.

He climbed onto his bed and sat down, cross-legged. Reaching around to the back of his neck with one hand, he felt for the longer hairs of his rattail. It hurt, but not much, to yank out a few. He brought his hand back around to see the result. Not all that long, really, but they would have to do. Carefully, he twisted three strands together for strength and tied the ends to form a loop.

After supper, Michael waited for the unicorn, sugar in one hand, golden loop in the other, but hours passed without any sign of it, and this would be the last night before the wallpaper was to come down.

He was beginning to feel sleepy when the unicorn finally stepped into the room and approached him. By now the unicorn trusted him enough to take the sugar right from his hand. It stretched its head forward to nibble the sugar, its lips tickling Michael's palm. Michael reached forward with his other hand and dropped the loop over the horn. Then, ignoring the magical jolt, he pushed it down until it was snug, near where the horn emerged from the unicorn's head.

The unicorn didn't seem to notice. It finished the sugar and turned to leap back into the wallpaper. Michael watched anxiously. The unicorn sprang at the wall . . . and its hooves struck a solid barrier, but it was unable to halt the momentum of the jump. The unicorn crashed to its knees with its head and neck twisted sideways against the wall. It struggled to its feet, shaking its head, then took a cautious step forward, neck outstretched. Its nose bumped the wall and it danced back, snorting and wild-eyed.

Michael hurried to the unicorn's side. He stroked its neck and tried to calm it, whispering, "It's okay, everything will be all right. I'm going to call you Spike, and I'll take good care of you, I promise. Come outside. There's some nice clover in the yard." Tugging at the unicorn's mane, Michael led Spike out of his room, but in the more confined space of the hallway, the unicorn planted his hooves and refused to move farther. "Shh, it's all right. Wait here," Michael said, then walked ahead and opened the back door. "See, it's better out there."

The unicorn took two halting steps toward him, then Michael flattened himself against the wall as the unicorn surged forward, bounded down the hall and through the door, and jumped over the steps onto the grass.

Michael showed it the patch of clover near the back fence, and the wild oats growing in the alley. He brought a pail of water, setting it behind the maple tree so his mother wouldn't notice. With luck, the unicorn's magic would make it invisible most of the time. Once Spike was chewing a mouthful of grass and clover, Michael went inside to bed.

That night, all his dreams were wonderful except one sad one near the end. It was too dark to see, but he heard a girl crying and calling out, "Dreams, Dreams! Where are you?"

He woke early for a Saturday morning and forgot about the bad dream in the rush to see his new unicorn.

"Hello, Spike," he said, stroking the unicorn's velvety nose. The unicorn nudged him, carefully keeping its horn out of the way. "I forgot," said Michael. "I'll bring you some sugar later."

Michael spent the day helping his mother strip old wallpaper and watching the unicorn through his bedroom window. After supper, he refilled the water pail and fed the unicorn two cubes of sugar. Touching the horn was still magic; the astronaut dream was the best so far. But there was a sad one again, longer than the last, and this time he was able to see an elf-child huddled under a tree, crying herself to sleep.

After a brief morning visit with Spike, Michael helped his mother put the mural up. The day was nearly over when he left his mother admiring it and went out for another visit. He sat down on the grass to watch Spike eat and struck a few sparks with the flint and steel. Spike started at one of the flashes, and Michael held out his birthday present. The unicorn sniffed it once, then turned listlessly away to eat a little clover, and Michael noticed that its coat didn't gleam as brightly as it had the day before. That night, the sad dream overshadowed the exciting ones, and Michael woke to find himself clutching the flint and steel so hard the flint had almost cut his palm.

His friends at school were much more impressed by his father's gift than Spike had been. Everyone wanted to try it. He passed it around before class and let Patrick try it again at noon, then tucked it back into his pocket for the rest of the day.

When he got home, he stuffed some sugar cubes in his pocket and went out to tend Spike. He gave the unicorn fresh water, then pulled out the sugar. The unicorn ate it all, trying to poke its nose into Michael's pockets for more. "No, no more. That's all I brought, see? There's nothing else in there." Michael turned his pockets inside out to prove it, and suddenly realized that there really wasn't anything else there. Not even the flint and steel. He got down on his hands and knees and groped through the grass for it, feeling cool blades but no pocket-warmed wood. He traced his steps back to the house, scanning the ground. Nothing.

He walked back to the school, but the farther he went without finding it, the harder he found it was to keep looking carefully, without hurrying too much. He had to run to be in time for dinner, anyway, and stumbled a few times from watching the ground for the flint and steel instead of where he was going.

Michael spent a fretful evening and went to bed without remembering to touch Spike's horn. His dreams were all dull and ordinary again, except the sad one, which was more vivid than ever. This time, the elf-girl almost seemed to be able to see him as she searched tearfully for whatever she had lost. Michael woke with a start in the middle of the night, still hearing her now desperate shout of "Dreams!" but he stubbornly put his suspicions out of his mind and went back to sleep.

He watched the ground all the way to school again, and searched until the bell rang, scuffling up the dirt wherever he could remember being the previous day, but with no luck. He was tired and found it hard to concentrate on his classes, even during the hour in the library.

At the end of the day, though, he went outside to find Carol, tough, obnoxious Carol Johnson, playing with his flint and steel. "Hey, that's mine!" he shouted, running up to her, reaching for his birthday present.

"Says who?" she asked, holding the object out of reach and hiding it behind her back.

"My father gave it to me. It was my grandfather's."

"So? I found it. It's mine."

"I didn't throw it away, I just dropped it. Give it back, okay?" Michael tried to grab behind her for it, but she backed up against the wall of the building.

"Get away from me, pukebreath," Carol said, shoving him with her free hand.

Michael fought the urge to punch her. He jumped as someone came up behind him and spoke. "Geez, Carol, what do you want that thing for? Come on, give him his present."

Michael turned to find Emily Tanner watching him and Carol. "What do you say, Carol?" she continued. "We'll be late for basketball practice."

Michael looked back at Carol. "Yeah, it's just a stupid baby toy," she said, then tossed the flint and steel onto the ground at Michael's feet and stalked away. "Come on, Emily."

As Michael bent to pick it up, Emily touched his shoulder and whispered, "I think it's cool that your dad's present means so much to you." She jogged off after Carol before she could see him blush.

When he got home, he found the unicorn standing in a corner of the backyard with its head hanging down almost to the grass, but it wasn't eating. "Dreams!" Michael shouted as he ran toward it. The unicorn looked up. "Yes, I know that's your real name." Dreams allowed a brief hug, and as it pulled away, Michael reached for the horn to slip the golden loop up and off. Dreams tossed its head and reared up, pawing at the sky. It thumped down, looking at Michael expectantly.

"Time to go back," said Michael. He opened the back door and led the way in. As he turned the corner into his bedroom, he stopped short, staring. There were no more fields or forest, only ocean. Michael groaned. "I forgot. Even if you can get through, you'll drown." He led Dreams outside, then ran back in to his mother's office.

"Mom, what did you do with the old wallpaper?"

"Threw it out, of course. Why?"

"I need it." Michael raced into the garage, but there were no trash bags there. Suddenly he remembered the bags that had been piled on the sidewalk when he left for school that morning and hurried out to look, but of course the garbage truck had been by hours earlier. He ran back into the house and was breathing hard when he leaned around the doorway of his mother's office again.

She looked up at him and frowned as she saw his face. "Michael, what's wrong?"

Ignoring her question, he asked, "Did *all* the garbage get put out today? Is there any left?"

She shook her head. "Of course there's none left.

Michael, are you sure you're all right? You look terrible."

Michael managed to keep himself from crying, but his voice shook as he said, "Never mind. I'm fine," and ran blindly outside again. He trudged back around the house, kicking dejectedly at the odd dandelion in the grass.

"This is all my fault," Michael whispered as he buried his face in the unicorn's mane. "I'm sorry, Dreams."

The unicorn bent its head down over his shoulder for a moment, whether in sadness or sympathy, Michael couldn't tell. He sat down on the back steps with his face in his hands.

"Will this do?" his mother asked him.

Michael jerked his head up. She was standing on the top step; Michael took the piece of paper she held out and saw that it read MICHAEL'S FIRST ROOM in big, black letters. He turned the page over and found a sample of his old wallpaper pasted there.

"I kept it in your baby book," she said. "I don't know what's wrong, but if this will help, you can have it."

"Thanks, Mom!" Michael jumped up to hug her tightly, then waited breathlessly until she was back inside the house. He held the scrap up against the wall of the house. Would it be enough? Was the magic still there? "Try, Dreams," he said. "See if you can get through."

Dreams pushed its nose up to the paper, but nothing special happened. The paper moved a little against the stucco with a scraping sound, and that was all. Dreams backed up, shaking its head and snorting; Michael pulled the paper away from the wall.

"I'm sorry," Michael said again. "I didn't think you'd be trapped here forever. I wish I could help." His eyes filled with tears; he blinked them back, but one escaped to trickle down to his chin and drip onto the paper in his hand. He jumped and dropped the paper, startled to feel a fragile tingle of power coming from it.

"Dreams, I felt something! Is there something I can do to make it work? Anything?"

Dreams looked at him thoughtfully for a moment, then reached its head forward and nibbled at the left sleeve of Michael's sweatshirt until it had a bit of cloth between its teeth. The unicorn tugged until Michael held out his hand, then let go.

"What is it? Do you want me to give you something? I don't have any sugar with me right now."

The unicorn shook its head, just slightly, then bent down and set the tip of its horn against the palm of Michael's outstretched hand. It tilted its head a bit to look Michael in the eye. Its stare was calm, questioning.

Michael trusted that stare. "All right," he said, then closed his eyes and swallowed.

The jab of pain made him gasp and cry out, and he couldn't help jerking his hand away. The tip had broken off and was embedded in his flesh. He pulled it out like a giant thorn; a large drop of blood welled up, then disappeared as the wound healed before his eyes, leaving only a tiny, round scar. He looked at the piece of alicorn; it was no longer than his thumbnail, and it was reddened with his blood.

The unicorn nudged his right hand, then bent its head to the ground and nosed the paper toward Michael.

Michael picked it up. "I closed the door, so now I have to open it, is that it?" he asked.

The unicorn tossed its head. It began to dance in place with its front hooves, back and forth, more and more excitedly.

Michael held the sheet up against the wall again. This time, he used the bit of alicorn to draw a line of his blood down it; the wallpaper crackled with power. "I think it's ready now."

The unicorn stretched its head forward and whuffled warm, clover-scented air into Michael's face. It backed up two paces, leaned back on its hind legs a little, leapt toward the scrap of wallpaper, and disappeared into it with a flash of light so sudden and bright that Michael had to close his eyes against the spots for several minutes.

When he opened them, there was nothing left of the wallpaper but a few charred fragments that could have come from anything. Dreams was gone. Michael bit his lip and clenched his fists, trying not to cry; something poked his right hand and he remembered the alicorn. Carefully, he opened his fist and peeked. Dreams had left the tip of its horn with him. It was no longer bloody, but crystal clear again.

Michael pulled the flint and steel from his pocket and tucked the piece of alicorn into the secret compartment. He went inside, wondering what he might see in his new wallpaper, and whether Emily Tanner believed in unicorns.

THE
DREAM-CHILD

- NANCY VARIAN BERBERICK -

Night-woven moon-child, running, running—
starlight spinning down your spiraled horn,
like frost chasing your sea-gray neck,
the white-maned curve, the bow-bent arch.
Wind sighs, loving your shoulders,
streaming down your back, and falls away;
wind in the cold night crying,
too slow to catch the wonder.

Speed-sparks leap from hoof and stone—
on the sea the waves are rising,
springing up to see the West-child,
the dream-child, the cloud-maned.
And your hard hoofs are drumming,
drumming, splashing up silver surf,
flinging sand back against the darkness
in sprays like diamonds, showering.

Bearded North is blowing,
his cold white breath steaming,
streaming, down the high stone places.
East is the day's bright face.
South is the world's heart, the unfolding warmth.
And West is where the black-eyed unicorn is running,
running on the edge of the world,
dancing down the road to home.

For the night is all spun, and this dream is all done.

THE
UGLY UNICORN

- JESSICA AMANDA SALMONSON -

In a garden in China one thousand years ago there was a maiden whose eyes were so pretty it was difficult to believe she was blind.

The blind girl's name was Kwa Wei. She was befriended by the Liu-mu, a homely silver-haired creature like a one-horned jackass. As Kwa Wei was blind, she had no idea the Liu-mu was ugly.

It came the first time in spring. Kwa Wei had been smelling orange blossoms and plum. On hearing the beast's hoofs upon the lawn, she thought it was a pony broken loose from Uncle Lu Wei's stables.

It was friendly, so she petted its head and felt the single horn, blunt at the end.

At once she thought it had to be a young Poh, the strongest and most beautiful unicorn of the many kinds that live in China. She clapped her hands and giggled.

"It's a Poh! Have you come to visit me in my darkness? I'm glad!"

The Liu-mu was too embarrassed and ashamed to say, "I am not the strong, good-looking Poh, but only an unfortunate Liu-mu." He had never been mistaken for anything beautiful until now. So all he said was, "Yes, I have come to visit you."

"Oh! How I wish I could see you with these useless eyes!" said Kwa Wei, and giggled anew.

The Liu-mu lowered his broad head until the blunt horn touched the ground. His eyes were as sad as a deer's.

"Would you like a ride through the garden?" asked the Liu-mu. Kwa Wei clapped her hands delightedly and climbed upon the ugly unicorn. "Hold on to my mane," he said, then trotted off through a maze of hedges.

Such creatures as the Liu-mu are able to run through more than one world. Kwa Wei knew at once that the garden had changed. The air was thicker with perfume. Grander flowers pressed near her at left and right as she rode around and about in Fairyland.

"Wheee!" exclaimed Kwa Wei, feeling the gentle wind in her hair. "Faster!" she said, laughing. "Faster!"

"Not too fast," said the Liu-mu. "I'll get worn out."

Such was the first meeting of Kwa Wei and the ugly unicorn.

The girl's uncle was a famous general under the rule of Duke Ling. Such important families live sad and violent lives.

On the day of Kwa Wei's birth, it had been arranged that she would marry Hah Ling Me, Duke Ling's grandson. When the girl was two years old, she became ill and lost her sight. She hardly remembered what it was like to see.

It was difficult to dissolve a marriage agreement between important families. If the marriage agreement were canceled, there might be war between Duke Ling and his own general. Year after year Duke Ling wished that Kwa Wei would die, in order that his favorite grandson needn't be burdened with a blind wife.

As for Uncle Lu, he knew it was a painful situation. Over the years he sought the aid of famous physicians from all over China.

"Her eyes are so beautiful," he said. "Why can't you make them work?"

The physicians could do nothing.

When his niece approached the year of marriage, Uncle Lu sent in desperation for the wizard-woman of Mount Tzu.

The wizard-woman was thin and tiny and wrinkled. She looked like an old fairy, that's how small she was. She had no teeth and her nose was so small you could hardly see it. She looked into Kwa Wei's face and in her eyes and finally said, "She can be cured."

Lu Wei was delighted. "Tell me how!"

"It requires only the rind of an orange and the pit of a plum, ground together with the horn of a Liu-mu."

Uncle Lu's spirits fell. "I have orange and plum trees

in my garden. They will bear fruit soon. But as to the horn of the Liu-mu, who has ever seen one?"

To Kwa Wei the little old wizard-woman said, "Pretty girl, would you like to be able to see through those eyes?"

"I cannot remember what it was like to see," she said. "The world is very nice even so." Then wistfully she added, "But I would like one time to see my friend the Poh, the most beautiful unicorn in China."

"Have you the Poh as your friend?"

"Yes I do."

"Well, you may go now. I must speak to your uncle in private."

When the blind girl left the hall, the wizard-woman said to Lu Wei: "There were silver hairs on her dress. They are the hairs of the Liu-mu. It may have represented itself as a glorious Poh, being ashamed of its ugliness."

From her bag of medicine, the wizard-woman retrieved two cubes of sugar. She said, "This is Liu-mu poison. The Liu-mu is intelligent and will not eat from the hand of anyone it doesn't know. Kwa Wei herself must feed the Liu-mu the poison. Then you can tear the horn from its brow and grind it with the orange peel and plum pit. When Kwa Wei eats biscuits made of this mixture, her eyes will be cured."

When the wizard-woman returned to her mountain retreat, Uncle Lu sat in his high-backed wooden chair and sighed. He said to himself, "I must let Kwa Wei believe the Liu-mu is a Poh. I must trick her into believing these poisonous cubes are sugar for her pet Poh. When the

Liu-mu is dead, I will take its horn to make the curative biscuits. But Kwa Wei must never know how it happened, or she will be unhappy. It is a sad thing, but if I do not do it, there will be war with Duke Ling."

Uncle Lu was not a bad man. Nevertheless, he planned to do this bad thing. Kwa Wei would have her sight; she would be able to marry her betrothed; no one would be offended, so there would be no war. What was the life of the Liu-mu, which after all was ugly, compared to all these good outcomes?

Even so, Uncle Lu felt terrible.

The following afternoon, Kwa Wei once more rode the Liu-mu in and out of Fairyland. "I smell a flower unlike anything in my uncle's gardens!" she said excitedly. "What does it look like, oh most beautiful and strong Poh?"

"It looks like a persimmon tree, but its flowers are lacy hollow balls that glow in the middle."

"Oh! And I smell something like a tulip tree, but it's different!"

"Its leaves are purple and red, but its flowers are emerald green."

"Is it true?" said Kwa Wei. "Fairyland is a beautiful place, intended for a unicorn as beautiful as you."

The Liu-mu felt guilty not to admit he was not a Poh-unicorn. To make amends for his lie, he said to the rider on his back: "I would like to take you to visit the Vale of the Unicorns."

"Is there such a vale?" asked Kwa Wei enthusiastically.

"The Vale of the Unicorns is terrifyingly beautiful, so much so that mortals go blind if they see it. As you are already blind, it will be perfectly safe. Even without your sight, you will feel the beauty, and smell the beauty, and hear the beauty of the Vale of the Unicorns."

Therefore the Liu-Mu took his rider toward two stone lanterns. The lanterns began to grow until they were as large as temples. Then Kwa Wei and the ugly unicorn were in the Vale of the Unicorns. The first unicorn they met was the fierce Hiai-chi. It was humming to itself—a primitive chant in a deep voice. If birds were as big as dragons, they might sound like the humming Hiai-chi.

"What is making such a deep song?" asked Kwa Wei, clinging tightly to the Liu-mu's curly mane.

"It is my friend the Hiai-chi. You can say hello to it."

"Hello, Hiai-chi. I have come to the Vale of the Unicorns riding the beautiful, strong Poh."

The Hiai-chi was a unicorn twice the size of an elephant. Its horn sprouted between the eyes of its dragon head. It had a tail like a hundred brooms and a mane like a lion. When this wonderful animal heard Kwa Wei say she was riding on a Poh, the Hiai-chi began to laugh in its bass voice. It said, "Are you riding on a Poh? Ha-ha-ha! You're a funny maiden!"

"Yes, I am the Poh-unicorn," said Liu-mu sternly, and the Hiai-chi stopped laughing.

"You have a marvelous voice to chant with," said Kwa Wei. "Will you chant sutras for my Uncle Lu, who has been unhappy for several days?"

"I will chant sutras for your uncle," said the Hiai-chi. Then Kwa Wei and the ugly unicorn went elsewhere in the vale. The next beast they encountered was the Kio-toan tiger-unicorn. It had striped fur and three pairs of legs. Its horn was like a licorice-and-orange candy stick. It was purring like a big kitten.

"What a pleasant sound," said Kwa Wei. "What sort of unicorn is it?"

"The tiger-unicorn, Kio-toan," said the Liu-mu. "If you reach over to one side, you can scratch one of its ears."

Kwa Wei scratched behind the Kio-toan's ear. The beast purred louder. "Such gentle hands!" said the Kio-toan. "Scratch a little to the left."

"I'm glad to meet you," said Kwa Wei as she continued to scratch behind the ear. "As I am blind, the beauty of the vale cannot hurt me. Even without sight, I can tell that it is a splendid place. And the tiger-unicorn is almost as lovely as the Poh that I am riding."

The Kio-toan laughed. "So that is a Poh you are riding? Well, thank you for the nice rub behind my ear."

The next unicorn they met was the Pih Sie, a little goat-unicorn with long white fur, golden eyes, and sweet pink lips. It made a sound like a gentle lamb and Kwa Wei guessed at once, "It's the Pih Sie! Oh, sweet little goat-unicorn, am I glad to meet you, riding as I am on China's most beautiful unicorn, the Poh!"

"That is very funny," said the Pih Sie in a musical voice. "That is funny indeed. This is the most beautiful Poh, is it?"

"Yes, I am," said the Liu-mu. "Don't pretend you don't know me."

"I know you very well, Master Poh, O Most Beautiful Among Us. But that ugly fellow over there among the peony flowers knows you better."

Among the peony flowers stood the actual Poh, a graceful horned horse with strength to devour lions. Suddenly the Liu-mu began to tremble.

"What's wrong?" asked Kwa Wei, feeling her friend shake.

The Poh called with the voice of an angelic being. "The Poh that you are riding is afraid because I am the vicious Kutiao, the leopard-unicorn. I am usually dangerous. But here in the Vale of the Unicorns, I am harmless. Don't worry about me, strong and beautiful Poh-unicorn, Ruler of the Vale of Unicorns. But as you leave, take care not to run into the ugly face of the Liu-mu, or your friend might not think the vale is excellent after all."

Then the Poh, pretending to be a leopard-unicorn, leapt across the hedge of peonies and was gone.

The Liu-mu, ashamed of itself, took Kwa Wei back toward the temple-sized lanterns. The two stone lanterns began to shrink until they were ordinary garden decorations. Then Kwa Wei recognized the sounds and smells of her uncle's garden.

"I am glad you took me to that place," said Kwa Wei as she climbed down from the back of the ugly unicorn. "The biggest surprise was the Kutiao. I never would have guessed a leopard-unicorn would sound like an angel instead of a grouchy old leopard."

"Kwa Wei," said the Liu-mu. "What if I weren't the most beautiful unicorn in China, but only an unfortunate Liu-mu that looks like a silly old donkey?"

"Ha-ha!" laughed Kwa Wei. "It could never be true, so why think about it? You are gentle and the best friend anyone could have. What could you be but the strong and gorgeous Poh? Anyway, you are the most beautiful to me."

Then remembering something, Kwa Wei opened the pouch dangling from her belt and removed two sugar cubes. She said, "Uncle Lu gave me these candies and said they would be a nice treat for my friend the Poh. Here, this one's your reward for taking me through the Vale of the Unicorns."

"Thank you, I accept," said the Liu-mu and ate the sugar.

Kwa Wei laughed musically and said, "I'm a selfish girl, so I'll eat the other one myself." She put it into her mouth. It was tasty but made her head swim. She said good-bye to the ugly unicorn and started away through the familiar garden.

When it was time for the day's meal, Kwa Wei did not show up at the table. Servants went to find out what she was doing. They discovered her on the ground outside the mansion, unable to get up. She was carried to bed and the local physician sent for. Uncle Lu Wei arrived to see what was wrong. Kwa Wei said, "Oh, Uncle, I don't feel very well. Do I have to eat my dinner?"

"Not if you don't want to," said Uncle Lu.

The doctor said, "It is something in her stomach. What did you eat today, young mistress Kwa Wei?"

"Nothing since lunch, except a piece of candy."

Lu Wei became pale when he heard this. He backed out of the room, stumbling. When the doctor came out, Kwa Wei's uncle said, "She has eaten Liu-mu poison prepared by the wizard-woman of Mount Tzu. What can we do?"

"She must have the antidote in two or three hours or she will die," said the doctor.

Soldiers employed by Uncle Lu Wei, along with everyone else available in and around his mansion, were sent immediately to Mount Tzu to search for the wizard-woman. Lu Wei himself went, it was so important.

Every afternoon, Duke Ling's favorite grandson, young master Hah Ling Me, visited the old ruler for a game of checkers. But today, the old man's favorite grandson hadn't come. When a servant went to check on Hah Ling Me and find out why he was tardy, he discovered an ugly unicorn stretched out on the floor of the young man's house. He was too sick to stand up.

Soldiers came and surrounded the sick animal and pointed spears at him. "What have you done with Hah Ling Me!" demanded one of the soldiers.

The sick unicorn said, "I am none other than Hah Ling Me, too sick to return to my human shape."

The soldiers weren't sure they believed it, but took the sick Liu-mu to the palace on the back of a cart. Duke Ling came out into the yard to talk to the Liu-mu. He recognized Hah Ling Me's sorrowful eyes and gentle voice.

"Grandfather," said the ugly unicorn, "as I was never allowed to see my betrothed, General Lu Wei's niece, I took this other form to see her in her uncle's garden. Now I am sick and cannot change back."

Duke Ling looked around at the members of his household, who were gathered in the yard to see the ugly unicorn. Then the duke announced the long hidden secret:

"My son Prince Ling, who died in brave battle ten years ago, had three wives. The favorite was Princess Chu who vanished after the death of my son. It was often rumored that the beautiful woman was a fairy princess and that she returned to Fairyland after the death of her husband. She left behind their only child, young master Hah Ling Me, a homely boy but so gentle and kind that everyone loved him. As you can see, he is a fairy-boy after all, and has fallen ill in his other shape as a Liu-mu. There is only one person with the skill to nurse a Liu-mu: the wizard-woman of Mount Tzu. All my soldiers and even the scullery maids and servants must go at once to Mount Tzu to find the wizard-woman in order to save my fairy-grandson."

*　　*　　*

Everyone from Lu Wei's mansion had already rushed into the mountains to seek the wizard-woman. The exception was one nurse who remained at pitiful Kwa Wei's side, mopping her brow with a silk rag. The girl moaned. Suddenly there was a commotion against the outside wall of the bedroom, as though something were trying to knock the mansion over.

The nurse hurried to a place beside the door to the hallway and grabbed a long wooden pole. She stood ready to fight. But when the wall crumbled, the nurse saw a big animal, China's most beautiful unicorn, its one horn long as a spear, its nostrils flaring, its four hoofs like big hammers pounding the floor of the bedroom.

The nurse dropped her fighting-stick and fell down in a swoon.

Kwa Wei sat up slowly and said, "Is it an earthquake? Why has the wall fallen in?"

Then Kwa Wei heard the huge footsteps and said, "Who is it?"

"You have met me once before," said the Poh.

Kwa Wei recognized the angelic voice. "You are the leopard-unicorn! You said you were dangerous outside the Vale of the Unicorns. Will you eat me?"

"I am not the leopard-unicorn, but the ruler of unicorns, the Poh that all call beautiful. I said I was the Kutiao because your friend the Liu-mu pretended to be me."

"My dear friend is not the Poh but the Liu-mu?"

"Now you know the truth. He is the ugliest of

unicorns. He is also sick, just like you, because you both ate poison. Come quickly! Ride upon my shoulders! I will take you to the only one that can save your life!"

Kwa Wei struggled from beneath the covers and went to the Poh's side wearing her silk nightgown. The Poh-unicorn knelt so that Kwa Wei could climb wearily onto the strong white shoulders. Then the Poh leapt through the hole in the wall and ran across the tops of trees.

Duke Ling's soldiers and servants and Duke Ling himself were all in the mountains looking for the wizard-woman, leaving behind one elderly gardener to stand over the sick Liu-mu. When the gardener saw the fiercely beautiful Poh running toward the castle right across the tops of trees, what could the old man do but hide in the bushes?

The Poh and its rider, Lu Wei's blind niece, landed gracefully in the yard. The elderly gardener trembled as he saw the Poh snatch up the Liu-mu in its mouth as a mother cat snatches up a kitten. Then the Poh ran off in the direction of a small stone garden ornament, where the Poh, the Liu-mu, and General Lu Wei's blind niece all disappeared.

Just like Kwa Wei's nurse, Duke Ling's gardener fainted.

Goodness! What a strange story! Does anyone know what is likely to happen next? The most beautiful unicorn in China, with the most ugly unicorn held by the scruff, and the beautiful blind maiden riding on its back, hurried into

Fairyland where the Poh deposited its cargo before the throne of the Fairy Queen.

The queen lived in a crystal palace. She was more beautiful than mortal words can tell. She kept at the side of her throne a small bag that looked exactly like the bag owned by the wrinkled old wizard-woman of Mount Tzu. Was it possible the withered-up mountain hag and the beautiful queen were the same woman? Who knows! In any case, the Fairy Queen was instantly able to cure Kwa Wei and the Liu-mu of the poison.

When the Liu-mu opened its eyes, it turned into the homely but sweet young master Hah Ling Me, Duke Ling's grandson. He looked up at the Queen of Fairyland and exclaimed, "Mother! I haven't seen you in so long I thought you must have died. I was sad!"

"You were meant for the mortal world, Hah Ling Me, and you were meant for this mortal girl. But your grandfather Duke Ling didn't want you to marry her because she is blind. With my tricks I have gotten you together. Now you will be married in Fairyland, where no one can stop you. You will be sent home with many wedding presents to start your own house and be independent of the families of Ling and Wei. You can do what you please from now on."

"And will you cure my bride of blindness?" asked Hah Ling Me.

"Fairies cannot undo what gods require. The only cure for her blindness involves your death, Hah Ling Me."

"I will gladly die for Kwa Wei!" said Hah Ling Me.

"Wait a minute," said Kwa Wei. "Have I complained because I'm blind? If I had my vision, you could never again take me to the Vale of the Unicorns, because first of all you'd be dead, and second of all, if I saw the vale with my eyes, it would blind me! I want to marry you, Hah Ling Me, oh most beautiful boy in China!"

"I am not beautiful, Kwa Wei, but you are very beautiful. Can you really marry such an ugly fellow?"

Kwa Wei laughed as though it were a joke. She said, "Let's get married right now."

Up on the side of Mount Tzu, the soldiers and household members of Duke Ling's palace had come to blows with the soldiers and household of Lu Wei's mansion. Scullery maids and stable workers and soldiers used their kung fu to give each other black eyes and bloody noses. After a while, they were all worn out. Their bones were sore. The fighters were scattered on the ground, sweating and puffing and unable to move. Duke Ling and General Lu Wei shouted for both sides to get up and fight some more. They finally did get up, but not to fight. Instead, a wonderful thing began to happen, and everyone stood to see it.

Coming down from the highest part of the mountain was a wedding parade of a startling kind. Riding on the back of the Poh were a groom and a bride. Hah Ling Me and Kwa Wei were both dressed in fabulous costumes and wore bright opera paint on their faces. Behind them came a whole train of animals with carts full of useful and valuable objects.

The Pih Sie or goat-unicorn pulled a cart laden with gold coins.

The purring Kio-toan or tiger-unicorn's cart was full of fine lacquered furniture, bolts of cloth that shimmered like precious stones and metals, and swords encrusted with gems.

The Hiai-chi or dragon-unicorn was humming the wedding song. It pulled a gigantic cart on which sat a big house with prettily carved doors and windows and roofs.

Walking alongside this procession was the old wizard-woman of the mountain. She had married them herself.

When the procession stopped, the wizard-woman said, "Hah Ling Me and Kwa Wei have been married in Fairyland. These gifts will set them up in their own house. It is for Duke Ling and Lu Wei to decide where the newlyweds' house will be."

"I will give my north acres, closest to Duke Ling's palace," said Uncle Lu Wei happily.

"I will give my south acres, closest to Lu Wei's mansion," said Duke Ling, equally glad.

Then the beat-up and bruised members of the two households began to dance and sing together. They followed the wedding procession down from the mountain.

For one thousand years this story has waited to be told. Now it has been.

STORY HOUR

— KATHERINE COVILLE —

"Where is he now, Grandma?"

"Who, dear?"

"The unicorn. The one you wrote the stories about."

"Why, he's in the books, I suppose." (Hush now! She's sensitive. She might hear you.) "Take my teacup, child, would you, and help me with these pillows?"

"Like this? Are you hurting? Should I go get Daddy?"

"Good Lord, no. Not Daddy. That's just fine. You're a good girl, Brooke. An odd one. Why aren't you out playing with your cousins, instead of sitting in this stuffy bedroom all afternoon with a sick old lady?"

"I like you, Grandma."

"Hmph. The whole family likes me, now that I'm on my deathbed. At least they like my royalties. Pack of buzzards."

"What are royalties?"

"Never mind, dear. Ask your father."

"But Daddy never answers my questions. You always do, Grandma. That's why I like you. You're interesting."

"Interesting? Well, I guess I've been called worse . . ."

"Grandma?"

"Yes, dear, what is it?"

"About the unicorn . . ."

"What unicorn?"

"You know! *Your* unicorn."

"Mine? What makes you think he's mine?" (Ha! More like the reverse. Do calm yourself!)

"The one in the stories, Grandma! Stop teasing!"

"Oh, yes. You like my stories."

"I *love* them. Aren't they true stories, Grandma? Aren't there really any unicorns?"

"Of course not!" (See the sparkle in those eyes! She reminds me of . . .)

"Are you laughing, Grandma?"

"How old are you, Brooke?" (So young! Wasn't I older?)

"I'll be eight next birthday."

"Eight. I'm past eighty now. How old do you think a person would be before they could tell what was real from what was not?"

"Daddy knows. He's always telling everyone. He told Aunt Helen that you live in a dream world. But aren't dreams real?"

"Some people's dreams are very real, child. Even their nightmares." (Could she have seen?)

"I have nightmares. Real ones. With goblins and awful crawly things in the dark. I scream and wake up."

"I should hope so." (It's started then. It must be nearly time.)

"But sometimes they're so very beautiful—the dreams, I mean. I dreamed I was in a forest all in colors that I don't know the names of. And tiny fairy people sat right on my hands and shoulders and head and let me be friends with them."

"Fairy people! Well, my girl! What a story that would make!"

"But Daddy said to stop talking like that or people would say I was crazy, like you. He said you were really crazy once, Grandma. What does that mean?"

"It means that your father has no imagination, dear. Now come closer. Sit right here on the bed with me, and I'll tell you a story; a real story, for you alone." (You must help me remember.)

"About the unicorn?"

"Yes, about the unicorn. And about a little girl—a lot like you. Maybe a little older."

"Was it you, Grandma?"

"Certainly not. Sit quietly now and I'll think of how it began . . ."

"It was a very long time ago. The little girl, Elizabeth, we'll call her. Lizzie, for short—"

"But that's your name, Grandma!"

"It's a perfectly good name, isn't it? Don't interrupt.

Now this little girl—Lizzie—had been ill for a long time. Her desperate family had tried everything, but she only grew sicker and weaker. Even sleep gave her no relief, for then the nightmares came, circling like wolves in the dark.

"One night it seemed that the nightmares would overcome her. Howling shadows clutched and dragged her down as if to squeeze the very breath from her body. Clammy fingers clamped tightly over her face. She could not wake up, or cry out."

"Like the swamp goblins! The horrid swamp goblins in your book!"

"Yes. Just like that. The creatures had almost pulled her down into their darkness when she cried out—not with her voice, for she couldn't—but with the very center of her soul . . ." (So dark . . . so cold . . . can't breathe . . .)

"Grandma? What happened? Tell me!"

"Then came the whiteness. Lizzie could see it even through her closed eyelids, bright and clear. It wrapped her all around with warmth, and laughter, and the scent of apple blossoms."

"Apple blossoms! That's what I smell!"

"You're imagining things, dear. That's very good. Can you imagine what the whiteness was?"

"The unicorn! He came to scare the swamp goblins away, and they all withered up like old dead leaves—"

"Yes, and they just blew away. Lizzie was not afraid any more. She looked up into the eyes of the unicorn. There she saw visions of things beyond her understanding, delight that could never be contained, and an ancient, untouchable sadness. He called her then—just as she had called him—and beckoned her to come away."

"And she went, didn't she, Grandma? Like the first book, where she rode on his back over moonbeams?"

"I really couldn't say. Her family said she had a good long sleep, that was all. When she woke up she was much changed. Her courage and her health had returned."

"Then it was only a dream? Didn't she ever see him again?"

"Oh, yes. She saw him many times, in many places; leaping off clouds, prancing about the school yard, playing in shadows on moonlit nights."

"You mean sleeping, or awake? Was she dreaming?"

"Sleeping or waking, she dreamed. She whispered all her secrets to him and showed him her treasures: her collection of precious stones from the drive; the magic swan feather she had rescued from the bird feeder; a secret potion she collected from the rain barrel. Sometimes they slipped away on long rides to unknown places. When they returned the girl would skip about, so full of wonderful secrets she thought she would burst." (Do settle down! How can I concentrate?)

"Elizabeth's family was worried at first by her whispering and daydreaming. Yet she seemed so happy and healthy they hadn't the heart to chastise her.

"Others were not so kind. After a time her childhood playmates outgrew their visions and set them aside. Lizzie's funny ways seemed to invite their mockery. She learned to keep her silence; to be on guard; to act like one of them. She ignored the prancing form in the clouds, the laughter on the wind. Eventually as she grew into a young woman, her thoughts strayed to other kinds of dreams."

"Do you mean like *love?* Like boyfriends? I would never want a boyfriend, Grandma. Not if I had a unicorn."

"Your day may come, too, child. In fact, she met a perfectly wonderful gentleman—a musician of great talent—and they fell in love and got married."

"—and lived happily ever after. Is THAT the end?"

"Well, they fell in love and got married. But their lives were very difficult. That was not the end.

"Her husband's music gave them great happiness, you see, but very little to live on. They sank deeper and deeper into troubles such as grown-ups must contend with, and children should be sheltered from. The day came when the beautiful music faltered—and stopped. Not long after that he was dead. Gone. And all of Elizabeth's worst nightmares came closing in on her."

"Was it the swamp goblins again, Grandma?"

"Something uglier than goblins, I'm afraid; things your father would call 'real': loss, hardship, betrayal, grief. They tore away at her like snarling jackals until her dreams lay all in ruins."

"What did she do?"

"Why, she called out—just as she had done so long ago—from the very center of her soul."

"For the unicorn?"

"Yes. He came for her, as she knew he would. He

promised he would never, ever leave her. They galloped off over the clouds and clear across time and space, until her heartache melted away, and she became a child again. Such joy! They reveled in all the old places, then galloped on and discovered new ones, kicking up stardust in their wake. Until they arrived one day at the cave of the Masked Enchantress . . ."

"The Masked Enchantress! I know that one! She gave a feast in their honor. A thousand birthday cakes, and ice cream that glowed in the dark! And the three-legged griffin came. And all the troll children."

"That's the one. And when they'd eaten all they could possibly hold—"

"—they threw their cakes at each other and sang rude songs. Grandma, that was the BEST story."

(Ah, yes. A child after my own heart . . .) "But that was not the end either, Brooke: They played and sang, it's true, until they all fell exhausted into sleep. But while they slept, a mountain of ruined cake and ice cream melted into a sticky river of mud, and inched their sleeping forms downward into the caverns. Shadows flickered in and out of their dreams like bats. Someone's cruel, shrill laughter echoed down from above them and collided with deeper echoes from below. The river oozed onward, downward into the inky void, until finally it slowed to a stop at the very bottom of Nowhere.

"It was a place without form or color, a place that had fallen through the cracks of time; the home of the goblin king. (Help me. I must remember . . .)

"After a while they woke up, still sticky, humming and laughing to themselves—when a terrible sound exploded in their ears. It was a voice.

" 'Silence!' it roared. They turned about, startled, trying to adjust their eyes. In the dim light, even the unicorn shone only in shades of gray. Around them appeared rows of dark figures, which seemed to have no faces. Somewhere beyond, a bubbling cauldron oozed smoke, making their eyes and nostrils sting.

" 'Is this how you show respect for your new king?' that awful voice demanded. From behind the cauldron lurched a strange, twisted form. More than monstrous, less than human, he was draped in tangled jewelry that looked to be made of the bones of small animals. An enormous crown of some sort towered over his head, but they could not see his eyes."

"Was it the goblin king?"

"Oh, yes. Yes, indeed. He drew close to them, until they smelled his rotten breath. Lizzie flinched, but the unicorn stood still—and unsurprised.

" 'The Masked Enchantress has served me well,' the goblin gloated. 'She has delivered to me this little mortal tidbit—and *you*, Unicorn. My ancient foe, called to life yet again by the trusting heart of a child. How touching. How *delicious*.' He cackled with something like laughter, and the shadow figures cackled back.

"It was then that the unicorn made himself heard. 'I have been betrayed before, Old One,' he answered. 'Many have sought the magic of my horn, but I have it still. Did you think I would bow it to you?' " (He should have known, the fool!)

" 'Your horn?' the goblin choked. 'What piddling magic should I work with your horn? Enslave a tribe of pixies perhaps? Stick their little wings together?' His grizzled face split into a leer as he sniggered at his own joke.

" 'You think,' cried the goblin, 'because I am hidden away from the world of men, that I do not know what is real? My beauties that you see here—all around you— they were men once. I did not enslave them. One by one, over the centuries they have come here and handed their souls to me; tired of the burden, you see. A pretty collection, is it not? Until now, I have had to content myself with these. Now, Unicorn, I need wait no longer. Now I will have the power to enter any human heart at will—MY will. Not theirs! The world beyond will be mine to plunder, and you—YOU—will be the one to give it to me.' "

"Grandma, stop! This is too scary. He couldn't really do that, could he?"

"It is only a story, Brooke. In any case, the unicorn would hardly allow such a thing, would he? I should think not."

" 'Bah!' the unicorn snorted. 'You are only a pathetic, heartless creature, who could never hope to share the heart of another. But come, Goblin, look into my eyes now, and see if you can enter there . . .'

"The goblin king threw up his arms and jumped back. 'You think you can trick me?' he cried. 'You think me pitiful? A fool? We shall see who is the fool now, my fine

GOAT, for my cauldron awaits! That sound you hear is a bubbling broth of horrors designed to break *any* human heart to pieces. My own recipe—everything from shattered dreams to undelivered love letters, with a few plucked pixie wings for flavor. I've kept the brew simmering for centuries, O Most Noble Unicorn, awaiting the last critical ingredient: your still-warm blood!

" 'Now seize them!' the goblin king commanded.

"The unicorn reared wildly, flailing and fighting, and Lizzie struggled valiantly, but the creatures came on in an endless, faceless sea. In the end, the unicorn lay in chains, and the girl looked on helplessly from behind cage bars. All was lost."

"Grandma, no! That can't be the end! Tell the rest!"

"We'll have no tears. Do you think happy endings grow on trees? I'm weary now, child. Give me some tea, and a little patience. I must collect myself." (Soon. Very soon.)

"Where was I? Oh, yes. All was lost—or so it seemed. But now Elizabeth called out to the goblin king with all of her remaining strength. 'There is no unicorn!' she cried. 'There never was a unicorn! There never will be! There never could be! There is NO SUCH THING!'

"The goblin rattled her cage, squealing and snarling, 'What is this? A trick? A trick? What do you mean? Tell me quickly or I'll eat you alive!'

" 'The unicorn was only a dream!' the girl cried. 'I just dreamed him up from my own imagination to distract me from my nightmares! He was never flesh and blood! You really are a fool—you and all your creatures—chasing after a girl's silly dream! You don't have to kill me! I'll die laughing at you!'

"The king turned and gasped, peering into the gray corner where the unicorn's chains lay empty. He did not see the girl's silent tears, or uncontrollable trembling . . ."

"But Grandma, he promised! The unicorn promised he'd never leave her! Where did he go?"

"Listen, child! Only listen! The unicorn had vanished. The goblin stood, stunned to silence. The faceless ones rocked in confusion.

" 'Perhaps,' the girl shouted at them, 'I imagined you, too!' And they cowered away from her, scattering into the shadows like vermin.

"Lizzie bowed her head heavily against the bars.

" 'I wish now,' she said, 'to hand you my soul, too, for I am weary of it.'

"The goblin peered into the girl's cage. She glimpsed his murky eyes now, filled with suspicion, and hate, and something else . . . and she shuddered.

" 'Yesss,' he hissed. 'Oh, yes. Mine forever . . .' "

"Stop, Grandma! Don't say anymore. This is too awful."

"Don't be silly, child. A mere fairy tale." (She must be warned . . .)

"But will she be all right?"

"She will be fine. She will be a corker. I should know."

"Okay, then."

"All right. Now the goblin opened the cage door and, grasping her by both wrists, pulled her close to his horrible face. 'This will be eeeasy,' he whispered. 'It won't hurt. You'll never feel any pain again. Just look at me! Look into my eyes and it will all be over. Just look. Look . . .'

"Elizabeth's wet eyelashes fluttered. Slowly, she lifted her head and, with a small sniffle, looked up—directly into the goblin's eyes. For an instant her heart looked directly into his. The smallest of smiles played at the corner of her lips. And then the goblin began to scream.

" 'The light!' he cried. 'A trick! A trick! He's given you the light!' The goblin king scratched and pounded at his own eyes as he fell writhing to the ground.

" '**GO**, mortal!' cried the king in his pain. 'Get away! Be gone!'

"For a moment she stood frozen, not knowing which way to run.

" 'Wait!' gasped the goblin, reaching blindly toward her. 'Remember,' he called, as she backed away, 'just remember this. You can flee from me this time, but you cannot fool me. You go ahead and find your precious unicorn. And when you do, I'll be watching! And listening! Do you hear? My servants will hound you ALL THE DAYS OF YOUR LIFE!' "

"But how did she find her way out?"

"I don't know, child. The way a thirsty animal finds water, I suppose. She sought clean air and daylight, and eventually she found them."

"So then did she go home?"

"Yes. She just walked—all the way back across time and space. She went back to her life and began again. She became a storyteller."

"Then it *was* you! And it was *true*! All of it is true, isn't it, Grandma?"

"It most certainly is not!"

"Then it's just a horrid old story, and I wish you had never told me."

"Perhaps it's not over . . ."

"Then she DID find the unicorn! He WAS true!"

"Brooke, listen carefully. There never was a unicorn, there never will be. There never could be. There is no such thing. Do grow up."

"But that's what Lizzie said, I mean you said, I mean —Oh! I . . . I think I might be growing up a little, Grandma. But it's so confusing!"

"What do you expect from a crazy old woman, then? Your father was telling you the truth, you know. Does that frighten you?"

"No, but . . ."

"Then come closer child, and hold my hands. We'll have a little game of Pretend."

"What . . . what are we going to pretend?"

"Why, anything you like! Now, look into my eyes. If you could imagine anything your heart desired, what would it be?"

"The unicorn, Grandma! I wish, I do so wish, that he would come to me!"

"Only imagine that you could call him." (Wait!

Listen!) "Call him like that other little girl did, from the very center of your soul. But first—"

"Unicorn! Come to me, Unicorn! I love you! I want to play with you! *Please* come to me! Come to me!"

"Brooke! You must listen!"

"Oh, Grandma! It's him! It's him! So white! So perfectly white and beautiful. It makes my eyes sting—"

"Oh, that's *fine* pretending, Brooke." (I told you to wait! It is too bad of you!)

"He's looking right at me, Grandma. Right inside me!"

"You have quite an imagination, child!"

"Oh! Yes! I really do! It's all so funny, Grandma! But sad, too. I want to laugh, but my eyes keep watering and my hands are shaking . . . I don't know what it is. My heart feels too tight."

(That, Brooke, is how you know that it's real.)

"Grandma? . . . I hear you just as if . . . what? How did you do that?"

"Some things, my dear, can only be spoken *with the heart*. Don't you agree?"

"Oh, yes. I do . . . but . . . how can I—Oh! Like this—" (Like this, Grandma? Can you really hear me?)

(Just exactly like that, my precious child. Do you see? Now your own heart will be his sanctuary, just as mine has been. It is the one place the goblins can never enter.)

(So that's where he went. He never left at all!)

(Oh, no. He kept his promise.)

(But you—Lizzie—she was so sad. She almost gave in to that rotten—)

(The goblin king was right about one thing, my dear. 'A trick! A trick!' It WAS a trick, and a fine one we pulled off, too, don't you think? Perhaps the old bully is a little more respectful now of a 'child's trusting heart.' Never know what it will shine back at you!)

(But how could you hold all that light inside? Didn't it feel like your heart might burst?)

(Yes. It feels tight at first, but it will grow, and grow. But Brooke, you must understand . . .)

(I know, Grandma. I think I do.)

(What do you know?)

(The dreams . . . If they're real—then the nightmares must be real, too, aren't they?)

(Only too real, dear. Remember the goblin king's words: They are watching still. And listening. Forever listening. You must guard your heart, and your tongue. You must speak of these things only as make-believe, a *story*, a dream. Do you understand?)

(It's all right, Gram. I understand. I'm not afraid, either. Not too much. I'll be SO very careful.)

(That's my brave girl. Guard your heart well.)

(But he's gone again, Grandma! Where is he now?)

(He'll be back, child, now that he's found you. Only now he waits for me. We must go for one last ride together.)

(Where will you go?)

(Not far. Only into the dream beyond this one. I think it must be the loveliest of dreams . . . I'm simply *consumed* with curiosity.)

"But Gram—!"

"My, you startled me child. I must have just dozed off. I get so tired now. And what have you been doing?"

"I—only daydreaming I guess, Gram."

"Well you know where that will get you! Perhaps you'd better go practice some addition, or conjugate some verbs."

"Grandma, stop teasing me now. Do you *have* to go?"

"Go? A sick old woman with rheumatism? How far do you think I'd get?"

"Not far?"

"Never far from you, child. Remember that."

(I love you, Grandma.)

(As I love you, and always will.)

"Do you want more tea now?"

"No, it's grown cold. I'll just rest a bit. Why don't you run along and play, like a good girl?"

"I will. Maybe I'll make believe that there are fairy people living in the garden! Friendly ones."

"You don't believe in that stuff, do you? A big girl like you?"

"Certainly not, Grandma! I am *way* too mature for that. I'm just making up a little story."

"Such an imagination! Where DO you get your ideas? . . . Now, kiss my old cheek and be off with you."

"I will."

"And, Brooke?"

"Yes, Gram?"

"Sweet dreams, my child. Sweet dreams."

THE
UNICORNS
OF KABUSTAN

~ ALETHEA EASON ~

Mikel stared through the large arched windows of the library, watching the snow fall. The fire cast a luster on the glass, which made the snowflakes look like glossy bits of gold dust falling from the sky. He was far away from the civil war tearing his country apart, the only one of his friends who was sheltered, and he felt like a coward.

The night was so quiet here in Kabustan, high up in the mountains. Mikel imagined he heard the sounds of the war through the branches of the fir trees, but he knew that the pounding of guns and the shriek of rockets were only inside his head. He had lived with these sounds for so long, most of his twelve years, that even now, safe in Omar's house hundreds of miles away, they were still with him.

The large oak door opened behind him. A stocky man with thick gray hair that fell to his shoulders walked in.

The blizzard had knocked out the lines to the generator, so he held a candelabra. Three candles were lit, and their bright flames added to the burnished tones of the room.

"I've been looking for you," Omar said.

Omar had never forbidden him to come into the library, but Mikel knew it was the one place in the house that was private. But on this night the doors had been left wide open, and his curiosity drew him inside.

Mikel was big for his age and could have been easily mistaken for a boy two or three years older. Though he had been here for two months, he hadn't noticed how much he resembled his host, how their eyes were the same shade of amber brown, how the frame of his body mirrored Omar's. This mysterious friend of his mother's did not force companionship upon him, but left Mikel alone for long hours as he pored over the books in this room.

To Mikel's surprise, Omar said nothing about his being there.

"Supper is ready. Are you hungry?"

"Yes, thank you." Mikel was about to follow Omar to the dining hall when the glass ball on the library table caught his eye. "That's strange."

"What?"

"The figure of the unicorn inside this glass. When I first came in, it looked tan. Now its coat is a rusty brown, and it seems bigger."

Mikel reached for the glass.

"Don't touch that!" Omar shouted, then quickly regained his composure. "The glass is very, very old. What you saw must be due to the light, Mikel. Come along, before the food gets cold."

When Mikel first arrived, the quiet of the mountain un-nerved him and any unexpected noise made him jump. When a hawk cried, he thought he heard the shrill timbre of a missile. A tree branch beating against his window brought back the memory of machine-gun fire in the streets. A door slammed shut, and Mikel dropped, expect-ing the blast of an explosion.

The last night he was in the city, his mother had awak-ened him and told him to dress quickly. She had bribed a truck driver to smuggle him out of the country.

"The driver will take you to a friend of mine who lives in Kabustan. His name is Omar, and he will take good care of you."

This was the first time Mikel had ever heard of this friend.

"You're not coming with me?"

"It would be too dangerous for both of us to travel. I'll try to come later. Now, don't protest. You're going, and that's that."

Since Mikel had no papers, the driver hid him under a mound of potatoes in the truck bed. The soldiers were lazy at the frontier and only prodded the pile of vegetables with the butts of their rifles.

Mikel was afraid to move, long after they had crossed. The truck finally came to a stop.

"You can sit up now," the driver yelled as he pitched

the potatoes off him. "You can ride up front with me. Hurry up, I don't have all day."

The trip seemed endless after that. They passed through towns that became smaller and more exotic the farther south they went. Finally, in a village tucked away in the foothills of the mountains, they found Omar waiting for them.

Mikel couldn't sleep and decided to study the unicorn in the glass more closely. After lighting the candle on his bed stand, he walked as quietly as possible down the big staircase to the library. Omar would not approve, but he had to look at the glass again.

He set the candle on the table. The glass caught its light; the unicorn looked as though it stood in a fiery lake. Mikel knelt down to study it and found that the figure had changed colors again. Its coat now appeared to be silver; but something else made Mikel catch his breath.

"You're in a different position," he whispered. "Your head was up before. Now you look as though you're grazing."

A pile of Omar's books lay upon the table. Omar had evidently been looking through them after dinner. The books were all old, written in strange languages. A ribbon marked a page in the thickest one; Mikel opened the book and found a faded sketch of a unicorn in a ball, just like the one on the table.

Break the glass.

Mikel heard the voice in his head. It spoke softly,

but he was startled at the power of the command. He slammed the book shut and stepped backward, about to bolt from the room, when the glass began to glow softly. He couldn't help but pick it up. The unicorn inside lifted his head and stared at him.

Break the glass. Free us.

"No!"

Mikel said the word, but a strong desire to do as he was bid flowed through him. He was compelled to release whatever was inside. He lifted the ball above his head. The glass grew brighter, hotter; his fingers, then his palms burned. A high piercing sound pulsated through the room, and Mikel threw the ball to the floor with all of his strength. The explosion knocked him down. The library windows blew open, and the room filled with wind so cold his teeth clattered.

A thick golden pool bubbled where seconds before a Persian carpet had covered the floor. The broken pieces of glass floated in it like shards of ice. From the middle of the pool, a unicorn's horn began to rise, a swirl of light that almost blinded Mikel. A muzzle followed, skirted with a beard of silver strands, then eyes, ears, neck; powerful shoulders and haunches emerged. Up the beast came. Sparks cascaded down his body from head to tail, illuminating the room.

The library was dark again, and Mikel found himself against the wall. The unicorn stood in the middle of the room and pawed the pool a few times. Golden liquid hung from his hooves like honey. He snorted, and his breath formed small clouds of fog. Raising his head, he looked at Mikel and then leapt out the window.

The tip of another horn began to rise from the pool. Another unicorn emerged, a shiny black one with a lavender mane. She bolted as the first. The rust-colored unicorn rose from the pool, and then the tan. Six in all came forth, mares and stallions both.

Mikel got to his feet and looked outside. The glory was in the field in front of the house, pawing at the snow, rearing up on hind legs, snorting, running in circles, celebrating their freedom. The first unicorn, whose horn glistened now with crystals of ice, looked at Mikel and lowered his head, and then within the next breath, ran toward the rim of fir trees. The glory followed, their hooves crunching softly in the snow. All of them disappeared into the dark line of trees.

Mikel closed the windows and knelt on the carpet. It was damp where the golden pool had been, but other than the shattered glass there was no sign of what had just happened. He began to pick up the shards, not knowing what he would do with them, when Omar appeared at the library door.

"What's going on in here?"

Mikel was still on his knees. "I'm sorry." Then he looked toward the window. "Omar . . ."

Omar put his candle on the table, knelt next to Mikel, and touched the carpet's damp fibers.

"How many?"

"Six."

"Do you know what you have done?"

"I'm sorry," Mikel said again, but Omar waved away the apology.

"I've been searching for years to find the key to release them." He put his hand on Mikel's shoulder. "Legends say the unicorns were imprisoned at the time men started to wage war. For centuries, the glass has been unbreakable. How did you do it?"

"They told me to break it." Mikel stood up and walked to the table. The book he had opened had turned to ash. "Why do I feel so afraid?"

"You had the choice to refuse them. You've unleashed a great power into the world."

"So what should I do?"

"Follow them, son."

Mikel and Omar tracked the glory through the forest. The snow was no longer falling, and the full moon wove itself through the evergreen.

The unicorns had come to rest in a clearing. The man and the boy stood at its edge and watched. Only the first unicorn seemed aware of their presence. He turned his head toward them, snorted, and lowered his horn to the ground. When he raised his head, sparks of gold and silver fell from its tip and then melted into the snow.

The unicorn bowed again. Mikel tried to walk toward him. Omar held him back, but, after a moment, let go of his arm.

Mikel sank to his knees in the snow with each step he

took. As he walked through the glory, the other unicorns ignored him. They smelled sweetly pungent, like apple cider and cloves. Mikel heard an owl hoot, and then all was silent except for the soft swishing of their long glossy tails.

He stood two feet in front of the large unicorn and looked into the blue-gray eyes. Taking off his right glove, he held out his hand tentatively, more shy than afraid. The unicorn stepped forward and nuzzled it.

"Do you belong to me or do I belong to you?" Mikel asked. "What do I call you?"

He received no answer to either question. Instead, the unicorn knelt. Mikel hesitated for a moment and then climbed on his back.

The glory gathered around the stallion, and the six animals lifted off the ground, rising like a constellation to the sky. They flew north and rose above the mountaintop. The forest lay far below like a dark lake with an uneven shore and stars clustered like clouds above them. They sailed over the range of mountains, crag after crag of white fingers piercing the sky.

Mikel lay on the unicorn's neck to warm himself and peered down through the darkness. He felt the muscles of the unicorn work as they flew through the frigid air. Power radiated all around him, and he became aware of the magnitude of his responsibility for breaking the glass. He grew dizzy. For a long moment he was afraid he would tumble into the chasms below, so he pressed harder with his thighs and wrapped the silky threads of the unicorn's mane around his hands. He shut his eyes as tightly as possible.

Do not be afraid.

Mikel forced open his eyes and made himself sit up. His fear was replaced by the beauty of the flight. The glory had formed a shape not unlike a star; the backs of each animal glistened under the moon. Sparks fell from their hooves as they cut through the dark sky.

The peaks gave way to rounded hills, and farther to the north, an immense plain stretched before them. They were flying to Mikel's home.

They flew a while longer before they reached the city. Once above it, Mikel noticed entire sections were without lights. They flew to the west. Gunfire popped in the darkness, and then a blast of red light snaked underneath the unicorns' bellies. The light exploded in a cluster of crimson fire.

The glory circled the perimeter of the city. The gunfire grew more sporadic. They continued flying, and on the third pass the entire city was quiet.

Mikel's mother and his friends were below them, and he wanted to land. He pulled his mount's mane toward the city, but the unicorn would not respond to his commands.

"I want to go down there," Mikel shouted.

Not yet. It is not yet time.

The words echoed off the moon. He did not want to hear their message, but their tone calmed him, all the same. The glory flew in a single line back toward the mountains. The gunfire raged again. Mikel turned and watched the lights of the city disappear behind them.

"I don't understand," he said, thinking his words would be carried off by the wind.

We are not ready.

Mikel stroked the silver hair on the unicorn's neck, sensing his patience.

Someday they will be ready as well.

Omar was waiting when the glory descended. The snow melted where they landed, and tiny shoots of grass pushed up through the frozen ground.

We will stay here.

Mikel slid off his mount's back, so tired he could hardly stand. Though he was big for his age, he let Omar take his hand and lead him back to the house. As they walked through the snow, he saw himself tend to the glory. They belonged to each other, but the unicorns required his courage. He dreamed of flying through the clouds, soaring once again under the stars, returning home with the peace of the unicorns of Kabustan.

Song for Croaker Nordge

~ NANCY VARIAN BERBERICK ~
AND GREG LABARBERA

ummer's throat tightened. Her eyes grew misty as she sang.

> *He turned his face unto the wall,*
> *And death was in him dealing:*
> *Adieu, adieu, my dear friends all . . .*

She stopped, swallowing back tears sure to come if she continued the sorrowful song.

Emma sat next to the fire, a shawl wrapped around her shoulders, her thin fingers covering her lips. She slowly lowered her hand. "Girl, with that voice I'd swear you were your mother, Lark, standing there. 'Bonny Barbara Allen' was her favorite. When she was younger I would always catch her singing a verse or two in the garden."

Summer bit her lip at the mention of her mother.

Emma looked toward Summer's grandfather. "Have you ever heard a sweeter voice, Croaker?"

"Not since Lark," Croaker said, his own voice deep and gravelly, like boulders grinding together. He coughed once, deeply, making the rest of his words rasp. "Anyway, what doesn't sound sweet next to me?"

Summer managed a smile. Everyone in the small English village called her grandfather Croaker because of his crackling, rumbling, voice. Not only did he manage a nickname from the villagers but he also had a reputation for being an odd sort. Rarely did he leave his small stone house—a house lined with books and filled with trinkets that almost looked magical, save for the dust that stole their sparkle. Often Croaker would spend entire days hunched over a leather-bound book at his desk, scribbling notes and whispering in a low grumble. When he did go out into the village it was usually to get some bread or cheese or tea, but most often he would stroll a few miles to the lake and stare out across the water, into the woods beyond, like a man waiting.

Waiting for naught, the villagers would say. Our crazy old Croaker Nordge.

Croaker stood and opened the door. A gust of autumn swept a small twister of leaves across the floor. "I'll get more wood for the fire. Summer, go on and practice the song."

As Croaker closed the door Summer let her voice rise and fall in the sweet melody her grandfather called *the* song. Though wordless, the song was nothing like the scales she repeated with her music teacher, when she used to live in America, but a hauntingly beautiful series of notes, rising and falling like the wind.

Emma rocked in the chair. Every now and then she would lift her hand a little or lower it, gently nudging Summer to the correct pitch. Near the end of the song Summer's voice faltered. It always did, in the same place. Emma straightened in her chair.

"Summer, you mustn't be so quick about reaching that highest note. Ease your way to it."

Summer frowned. She liked singing the old ballads, like "Bonny Barbara Allen," much better than she liked singing this song of Croaker's. No matter how hard she tried someone always told her she never sang the song quite right. She plopped down in the easy chair next to the fire.

"Why does Croaker insist I sing the song over and over? And he expects me to do it perfectly."

Emma folded her hands in her lap and rocked back and forth. Though the old woman looked straight at her, Summer knew Emma's mind was someplace else. "When Lark was younger, about your age, she could sing almost as well as you. When she sang the song it filled Croaker with a magical sort of hope."

Summer turned away, chilled and suddenly aching. She understood hope. And she knew the pain it could bring. Before she came to live with Croaker, she and her mother had a farm in upstate New York with beautiful rolling hills and horses.

Until the sickness.

It didn't take long for Summer's mother to waste away, though Summer hoped, hoped that the doctors would find a way to save her.

They never did.

Emma sat staring at the fire, perhaps lost in a memory of Lark. A bitter numbness filled Summer's chest, and she thought: Hope is for fools.

Summer rose from the chair and walked around the cozy living room, running her finger across dusty books all crowded together on low shelves. She picked up a small crystal from Croaker's desk and twirled it in her fingers. Firelight glinted off its rough-hewn edges. As she replaced the bauble she noticed the leather-bound book open on the desk, the one that Croaker scribbled in so intently. She picked it up and read: *She must have a voice, and a heart, clear and pure, each note of the Summoner's—*

Wind whistled through the house as Croaker opened the door. His eyes opened wide and he dumped an armload of firewood across the floor. "What are you doing with that book, girl?"

Summer closed the book and clutched it to her chest as Croaker darted toward her. She gasped as he snatched it out of her hands.

"You're not ready to see what's in here," Croaker scolded.

Emma rose from her chair and placed her hand on Croaker's arm. "Don't scare the poor child. You know she meant no harm."

"I'm sorry, Croaker," said Summer. "I just thought there might be more songs in there, that maybe you were writing them down for me so I wouldn't forget."

Croaker coughed, then pressed his hand to his mouth, as though to hide it. Wordless, he walked from the room.

Summer lay on the floor in front of the fire, reading a book of English myth and folklore. For the last week she had been studying the topic in school and when Croaker found out he hustled her to the shelves and enthusiastically pulled off book after book, taking delight in pointing out magical tales of King Arthur and his knights, of dragons and beasts of legend.

Summer wasn't the only one studying. Ever since she began reading the folklore she had noticed Croaker thrusting himself deeper into his leather-bound book, as if he were an adventurer readying for a quest.

Now she closed her book and put another log on the fire. Croaker dozed in the easy chair, his glasses resting on his lap. Summer guessed he must be tired from their trip to the lake earlier in the afternoon. Even Emma, who usually stayed for tea, had gone home, jokingly complaining about aching bones and creaking limbs.

Stretching and yawning, Summer eyed the leatherbound book sitting on her grandfather's desk. Why was Croaker so secretive about that book? What kind of mysteries were hidden in there? And why didn't he want Summer to see them?

Convincing herself the book held more songs like

"Bonny Barbara Allen," that he just wanted to surprise her someday, Summer quietly picked up the book and opened to the middle: *The unicorn is a secretive beast, one that will come only to the call of a maiden. She must have a voice, and a heart, clear and pure, each note of the Summoner's Song flowing through her like she was an instrument of magic. If her heart is true, and the song is rightly sung, the unicorn will appear out of the mist and bow to his summoner.*

Summer's heart fluttered. Flipping through the pages she read all kinds of notes and poems and legends about unicorns, written in Croaker's squarish capital letters. Croaker grunted and opened his eyes. As soon as he saw Summer with the book he bolted upright in the chair.

Summer stiffened, ready to be scolded again. Her grandfather gently reached out his hand. "I guess you would have to know sooner or later."

Summer lowered her gaze, her face warming, and placed the book into his hand. Croaker motioned to the rocking chair and Summer sat down, sliding it closer to her grandfather.

In a low voice he began, "Have I ever told you how much I love the unicorn? It has been in our tales for centuries. But many don't know what they're really about. This book," and he tapped the soft leather cover, "this book holds everything I know about unicorns, a lifetime of lore. Did you know that the unicorn's horn is made of finest pearl and his breath smells of flowers in a morning meadow?"

Summer shook her head and opened herself to the story and the legend. The fire crackled and warmed her back.

Croaker continued in a raspy whisper. "Many don't know the unicorn's tail is tufted like a lion's or that he has cloven hooves, like a deer—hooves that never leave a mark of his passage. Oh, what a fine beast a unicorn, so full of grace and mystery."

Smiling, Summer leaned forward.

"Your mother, Lark, had a beautiful voice. She could make a nightingale fly away feeling unable to compete with her song. If she'd practiced harder I believe she could have used her voice to summon a beast of legend. How I long to see a unicorn, Summer."

Summer's smile melted away. Wary now, she remembered what she had read: *If her heart is true, and the song is rightly sung, the unicorn will appear out of the mist and bow to his summoner.*

All the things she had heard the villagers say about "crazy old Croaker Nordge" came crashing in on Summer. She drew her knees up under her chin and wrapped her arms around her legs. She huddled in, shutting out the possibility that the villagers were right about her sweet but unusual grandfather. With her lips trembling she asked, "What are you saying, Grandpa?"

"Your voice, Summer. Don't you see?"

Summer feared she saw all too well. "Croaker, are you saying you want me to sing you a unicorn?"

Croaker grinned, showing crooked teeth. "Yes!" he cried. "Yes, Summer!"

Summer bolted up from the rocker and said, "Why didn't you tell me?" She clenched her fists and her body shook. "How could you do this to me?"

Croaker held out his arms, pleading. "What, dear? Do what? I thought you'd want to help me, to be there, to see a unicorn."

Tears welled up in Summer's eyes, tears mixed with anger and sadness. "How could you trick me into singing that Summoner's Song? How can I ever sing it again without feeling foolish?"

"But, Summer, your mother, she loved the song. She just—"

"My mother's dead, Croaker. I'm not her, and I'll never sing that song of yours again. It's true, what everybody says about . . ."

A look of pain crumpled Croaker's face, as if someone had punched him in the stomach. "What's true, Summer? What . . . ?"

Summer turned and ran out the door.

She ran through the village, the smell of evening fires thick in the air. She pressed tears from her eyes with the back of her hand as she passed in front of the baker's shop and the pub, making her way to Emma's. When she reached the door she didn't even bother knocking. Bursting into the house, she panted, "How could you, Emma?"

Startled, Emma turned from the oven, a tray of warm cakes in her hands. "How could I what, dear?"

"How could you let my grandfather make me sing that song? You went right along with him. Why would you let him believe I could call a unicorn from out of nowhere? Do you think you're doing him a favor by keeping his hopes up, by pretending to believe in this craziness as much as he does?"

Emma put the cakes on a dish and sat down at the table. "Who says I'm pretending, dear?"

"You're not telling me you actually believe in unicorns?"

The light of the kitchen hearth-fire dressed Emma in gold. "What difference would it make if I said I do?"

Summer shook her head. "Because it's cruel to go along with Croaker, to make him believe, to keep him . . . hoping."

Emma poured two cups of tea. "Look who knows so much about hope. You've barely thirteen years behind you and already you're so wise about it. And I suppose you have nothing to hope for, nothing to dream about?"

Summer slumped into a chair and stared into her lap. "The only hope I ever had left when my mother died." She couldn't meet Emma's eyes when she whispered, "And Croaker is as crazy as everyone says if he hangs his hopes on seeing a unicorn."

Emma, her blue eyes soft with memories, said, "Child, our Croaker has dreamed of seeing a unicorn all his life. Don't you see how much his heart is in this? What harm would it do to try for him?"

Her throat tightened, and Summer couldn't answer. This talk of hope made her want to cry for missing her mother. Just when she thought the tears would spill, Emma stood up and hugged her. "Do you believe in magic, Summer?"

Summer closed her eyes, trying to hide from memories of her mother, of that dark time when sickness had eaten her down to bones with skin stretched around them, how nothing, not even hope, could save her.

"No," she whispered. "I don't."

Emma held Summer's face in her hands. "Well, I do. I hear magic every time you sing, as if you were an instrument the wind itself played. Do you think Lark named you Summer after the season? No, girl. She named you *Sumner*, but when you were a child learning your name your little lisping tongue could only manage Summer and so we all called you. But your name is Sumner, and in the old speech it means the Summoner."

Summer looked into Emma's eyes, steeling herself against Emma's appeal. It was all nonsense, this stuff about myths and lore and who named her what.

"He loves you, Summer."

Summer couldn't steel herself against that, for it was truth.

"All right," she said. "I'll sing the song. Not because I believe it, but because Croaker has been good to me. I owe him that."

Emma said nothing, only tenderly patted her cheek.

Summer stood at the edge of the misty morning lake, feeling as if she were on a fool's errand, getting ready to summon a unicorn from the woods beyond. No one could ever expect a song, or anything, to do that. This was no fairy tale, but the real world, where your mother dies no matter how much you hope.

Summer had lived with hope's lies for too long, a knowledge Croaker didn't understand. As much as it pained Summer, she had to prove it to him.

With startling suddenness a bright blue kingfisher slipped from the sky, cut low over the water to pluck a fish from the shallows. When the water became still again, Summer looked toward Croaker. He coughed once, hard and deeply in the cold morning air, his breath coming in small tufts of steam. Then he nodded sharply.

Summer began softly, moving up and down the notes as her grandfather taught her, trying to sing them as clearly and perfectly as she could. A light sparkled in Croaker's eyes, a light of hope that pained Summer to see. No matter what anyone hoped, she knew with all her heart that a unicorn would never come.

She sang louder, her voice reaching the perfect pitch, piercing the brisk morning. She even reached the highest note, the one that always made her falter. When this didn't work, no one would be able to say it was because she didn't do it right.

The song ended and silence surrounded the glade. Croaker held his breath, his head tilted slightly back, his gaze riveted to the woods on the other side of the lake. They stood that way, in the silence, for a long while, Croaker never taking his eyes from the woods.

Finally Summer placed her hand on his arm. "Grandpa?"

A small tear trickled down Croaker's cheek.

Summer whispered, "Let's go home, Grandpa."

He coughed, hard. Wheezing, he leaned on her arm, suddenly old.

For days Croaker sat silently in the rocker, staring at the fire. Summer would place breakfast and dinner in front of him only to take the plate back a few hours later, most of the food untouched. The times Emma came to visit, Croaker would shoo her away with a wave of his arm and a hoarse grunt. Summer didn't try to talk to Croaker, believing it would be easier for him to get over his disappointment if she left him alone.

But she did worry.

Many times she went to Emma and told her how the light had gone from Croaker, how his enthusiasm for his legends and the leather-bound book had disappeared, and how his cheeks had sunk in from all the days of not eating. She feared he was dying. Dying of a broken heart. Dying because no unicorn came.

Dying because she had sung his song not to bring hope but to kill it.

A cavernous hole opened in Summer, swallowing all the light in her life, leaving behind the terrible darkness she hadn't felt since her mother lay dying. Croaker was all she had left. He couldn't leave!

She bit her lips together, trying to keep from crying.

If only she could bring him back, call him from death. But the only way to save Croaker was to sing him a unicorn. What good would it do to—

Then she remembered the book, the passage she had read. *If her heart is true, and the song is rightly sung* . . .

A spark of light flickered inside her. Summer trembled when she began to do what she never thought she would do again—hope. It pained her to dare think such magic existed, but she was Croaker's only hope. So Summer gathered her courage. With her voice and her heart she'd call a unicorn. It was the only way she knew to save Croaker.

"Croaker, let's go back to the lake. I can do it this time. I can sing you a unicorn. You have to let me try. Please."

Croaker humphed and said, "I won't be wasting my last day on that, child. I've wasted most of my life already."

Desperately, she cried, "How could you say that? You can't let your dream slip away. I'll sing again, and I'll do it right. I promise! Isn't it worth one more song, Croaker?"

Croaker stared into the flames, his gaze and mind far away. Finally he said, "Go get Emma. And fetch my coat, Summer."

Croaker leaned on Emma's arm. They all stood in the glade, staring out over the lake, mist floating like a dream across the water.

Summer didn't hesitate. She drew in a deep breath and

sang the Summoner's Song. She closed her eyes and let the notes rise and fall. Her heart pounded as she thought about Croaker, about how she hoped he would be okay if by some miracle a unicorn would come. In that hope the song took on a life of its own. Summer drew in another breath and felt as if her spirit flew from her body. Music flowed through her as if she were a flute and wind the player.

The last note faded and the song ended.

Her eyes still closed, Summer rocked back and forth, still caught in the web of the song.

For a long time they waited in silence.

Then in the distance an echoing, like the far flourish of a herald's trumpet.

Summer opened her eyes and saw a flash of silver-white through the trees. All around magic floated on the air, tiny sparks of dancing light.

Croaker fell to his knees. Emma gasped and cupped her hand over her mouth.

A unicorn emerged from the woods, prancing around the fringe of the lake. His coat glowed in the sunless morning. Mist swirled round his spiraled horn.

Summer knelt next to Croaker. Light had returned to his face. He hugged her and said, "You did it, girl. You sang the magic."

Summer held her breath as the graceful beast trotted to them. He tossed his head and whickered, prancing a tight circle that stopped in front of Summer. There he bowed to the Summoner, gently laying his horn in her two hands.

Summer reached out and stroked his mane. It felt like silk, his horn like smoothest pearl. "You're right, Grandpa. His breath does smell like flowers."

Tears flowed down Croaker's face as he took Emma's hand, reached out, and touched the unicorn's horn. "Emma, he's real. Isn't he?"

"Why, you dear old fool, what a time to start doubting."

The unicorn jerked his head up and down a few times then knelt in front of Croaker.

Summer's heart leapt. "I think he wants you to ride him, Grandpa. He wants you to ride!"

Croaker said nothing. Softly, Emma sobbed. Summer's smile faded when she saw the look on Emma's face, the pallor of her cheek. Slowly, afraid, she turned to Croaker and saw the truth.

Death was in him dealing.

Summer rushed to her feet and threw her arms around the unicorn's neck, crying, "No, please! You can't take him. I summoned you. Now he's supposed to get well and stay here with me."

The unicorn nuzzled Summer's shoulder and face as if he were trying to tell her he understood. But how could he understand that Summer's life without Croaker would be like a moonless winter night?

"No!" she sobbed. "Please. Please don't take him."

Whispering words meant to comfort, Emma pulled Summer away.

Croaker used all his strength to climb onto the

unicorn's back. When the unicorn stood, Croaker sat proud and tall, his hands holding the silvery mane. "It's the way it has to be, child. Teach your children the Summoner's Song and when it's your time we can be together again."

Summer wrapped her arms around Croaker's leg. "Please, Grandpa, please don't go."

With gentle strength, the unicorn turned, breaking her hold. He trotted away, and Summer's arms fell, empty, to her sides. Shaking, wrapping her arms tightly around herself, she watched her grandfather and the unicorn fade into the mist.

"Good-bye, Croaker."

She turned, saw tears twinkling down Emma's cheeks. Now she remembered the way Croaker used to cough, almost secretly, even before she'd first tried to sing the magic.

"You knew he was dying, didn't you, Emma?"

"I knew, child. And you gave him the best of gifts before he left. You made his hope real." She stooped, bending with the stiffness of age, and plucked something from the ground. "And I think a gift has been left for you."

Emma took Summer's hand in hers and loosely wound a long strand of silky hair round her fingers. Silver, the strand, and it glowed with light that defied the mist. Somehow Summer knew that, even in the darkest winter night, she'd be able to see the luminous strand of the unicorn's mane.

Emma put her arm around Summer's shoulders, turning her from the lake, guiding her toward the village.

"I'll take care of you, girl. You'll be all right."

Summer knew that what Emma said would be so, for she had the unicorn's gift.

Like hope, she thought, pressing her hand to her heart, her tears running freely now. This gift will shine best when light is least.

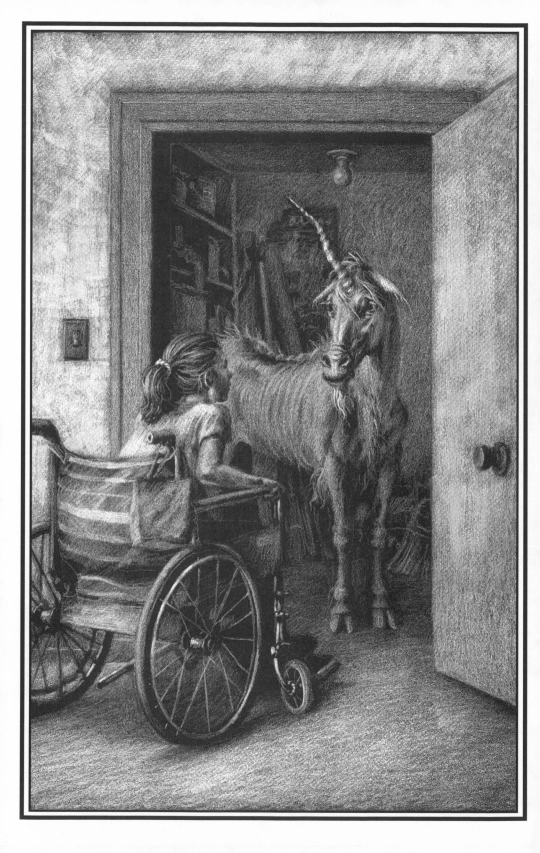

THE
HEALING TRUTH

~ KATHRYN LAY ~

Crystal pushed her wheelchair against the heavy doors that led to the school auditorium. She didn't know why she'd signed up for Drama Club, except that everyone kept telling her she was such a convincing liar she should use it for something.

"Welcome to the most exciting club at Davis Middle School," Mrs. Gray called from the foot of the stage. "Please, join us."

Crystal rolled down the aisle and over to the kids sitting in chairs placed in a half-circle facing the drama teacher. She stopped next to her best friend, Janna Carpenter. Crystal glanced around at the other kids. Although she knew some of them from her classes, most were in seventh or eighth grade and had probably been in the Drama Club before. They clustered together in small groups, sometimes snickering when they glanced at the sixth graders.

Mrs. Gray smiled. "I'm glad so many signed up for the club this year. How many of you have had experience on stage?"

All the seventh and eighth graders raised their hands, then stared at the sixth graders and shook their heads. Crystal folded her arms and puffed up like a bullfrog.

"Some of you new students must have had a *little* experience," Mrs. Gray urged.

One boy slowly raised his hand before dropping it quickly to his side.

Mrs. Gray pointed to him. "Yes? Your name, please?"

"Um, my name is José . . . José Rodriguez, and I played an angel in a Christmas play when I was seven."

The older kids laughed. "Ooh, how sweet."

Mrs. Gray shook her head at them. "That's enough." She turned back to José and smiled. "I think that's wonderful. Every experience in front of an audience is important."

Crystal glared at the snooty kids who nudged one another and whispered loudly. *They think they're so wonderful. I'll give them something to whisper about.* Her hand shot into the air.

"I've had lots of experience acting," she shouted.

Janna groaned.

Mrs. Gray smiled. "Really? Tell us about it."

Crystal took a deep breath. "Well, when I was in fourth grade, we lived in California—near Hollywood— and this director . . . I won't say his name, except that he is really BIG, you know? . . . Anyway, he saw me at the mall one day and told my mom to take me to his studio. They asked me to do a screen test and, well, I got to be in several movies. Course, you probably wouldn't recognize me . . . they made me wear wigs and makeup."

She glanced at the other kids and grinned. "I guess I wasn't on *stage*, like plays and stuff, but it's still acting."

"My, that is exciting," Mrs. Gray said. "I'm sure you can give us some pointers."

Crystal stared at the teacher and searched her face for a hint of what she really thought. Did Mrs. Gray know she was lying? Would she give her a little speech after the meeting about truth? Or would she ask Crystal to find another club to join?

A muffled laugh echoed around the stage. Crystal recognized Tracey Hammond, one of the eighth-grade girls from her P.E. class. Tracey stared at Crystal a moment, then whispered something to the boy next to her.

He grinned and pointed at Crystal. "Yeah, you're right, that *is* the girl, the one they say couldn't tell the truth if it did a tap dance on the end of her nose."

Crystal's face burned. She glared at Tracey, who gave her a tight-lipped smile.

Mrs. Gray cleared her throat. "Quiet, please. I want to discuss the first project we'll do this year. How many of you know what a soliloquy is?"

"I do," Tracey shouted. "It's like a long speech that one person gives. There's some in Shakespeare."

"Correct," Mrs. Gray said. "I think there's a lot of potential in this group for some exciting moments on stage, but before we decide on a production for the spring play, I would like each of you to perform a five-minute soliloquy of your choosing."

She walked up the stairs and across the stage, sweeping her arms toward the ceiling. "It can be dramatic, sad, or humorous. It can be something already written in a play or book, or something you compose yourself. This will be only for one another, so don't panic. We'll do them a week from today. It's your chance to decide if you want to continue in the Drama Club or not."

Everyone began talking at once—to Mrs. Gray, to one another, and to themselves. Crystal half-listened to Janna's chatter about the project. A speech? About anything? Well, she'd tell them a story they'd never forget. They'd expect something she made up . . . a lie, so why not give it to them?

"Crystal, there is a small box of old scripts in the supply closet beside the stairway," Mrs. Gray said. "Would you mind getting them while I pass out a list of suggested ideas?"

"Okay." Crystal rolled her chair around the group of kids. She passed the group of eighth graders bunched together.

Tracey whispered, "Make way for the Princess-of-Make-Believe."

Crystal thought about rolling her wheelchair over Tracey's pink high-tops. Instead, she pushed her way to the supply closet under the stage, bent forward, and grabbed the door handles. She yanked them open and came face-to-face with a unicorn of extreme ugliness.

"Mrs. Gray!" she shouted. "There's a unicorn in the supply closet."

Laughter echoed through the auditorium. Crystal stared at the creature, then leaned back to look at the drama teacher.

Mrs. Gray peered over her bifocals. "Crystal, if you can't find the box, just say so."

"But, Mrs. Gray, I'm not kidding. There really *is* a unicorn in here. Wow, is he ever ugly."

With a sigh, the teacher walked across the stage and over to the closet. She slipped in beside Crystal's wheelchair and pointed. "The scripts are in that box . . . the one marked SCRIPTS." She reached around the unicorn's shoulder and pulled the box from the shelf.

Crystal glanced at Mrs. Gray, who walked away without saying a thing about the mottled gray animal kneeling on the closet's wide floor, his shabby, crooked horn pointed toward the ceiling.

Crystal motioned for her best friend to come to the closet. "Janna, do you see anything on the floor?"

Janna nodded. "Dirt. Yuck, I think the janitor needs to clean this thing out."

"You don't see anything else?"

Janna shook her head. "What am I *supposed* to see? The president, come to give you a medal? A spaceman wanting your autograph? Come on, Crystal, I'm your best friend. You don't have to make up stories with me. We're in middle school now . . . and, well, you've got to grow up." She glanced around the room. "Tracey is looking at us. *Please*, please don't embarrass me in front of her. She knows *everyone* at this school."

Crystal watched the unicorn, wishing he would disappear and praying he wouldn't. She stretched a hand forward, wondering if she would feel only air if she touched him.

Her fingers stroked the curve of his cheek until he trembled and closed his eyes. Warmth shot through her, filling her with mixtures of sorrow and joy. She pulled her hand away, staring at the glow on her fingertips until it faded. The warmth left. She wanted to cry.

Rolling her wheelchair away from the wide doors, Crystal glared at Tracey and chewed her lip against the threat of tears. "I'm *not* making anything up, not this time. There's a unicorn in there and if you can't see him, well, you're just stupid. Excuse *me* for embarrassing you."

Crystal returned to the front of the auditorium and tried to come up with an idea for her speech, but all she could think about was the sickly-looking creature in the closet. She tried to ignore the giggles from the other kids. Even the other sixth graders were whispering together, sometimes stopping to glance at her.

She looked back toward the closed doors. Had she made up so many stories that she was beginning to believe in them, to see things that weren't really there? Maybe he wasn't really a unicorn, but a horse or a goat. But why would a goat with a horn stuck to his head be sitting in the supply closet? No, it was a unicorn. And he was real, she knew it, as much as she knew she had to see him again.

More than anything, she wanted to believe. A real unicorn, and *she* had discovered it. But why didn't Mrs. Gray or Janna see him, and what *was* a unicorn doing in the supply closet? And why wasn't he beautiful, like the delicate china unicorns she'd seen in the mall?

When the meeting ended, Crystal hung behind, pretending to look through the few plays in the box.

Mrs. Gray picked up her briefcase. "Crystal, the meeting is over. Just take the box with you."

Crystal threw the scripts back in the box. "I don't see anything here I can use. I'll just put this back in the supply closet."

Mrs. Gray waited. *Go away*, Crystal silently pleaded. Then, as if on cue, an office aide came into the auditorium and handed Mrs. Gray a note. She read it before stuffing it into her sweater pocket. "I've got to go to the office a moment. When I come back, I need to lock the closet."

Crystal bit her lip to hide the smile. "Yes, ma'am." When Mrs. Gray had gone, Crystal rolled back to the closet. It took a moment of maneuvering before she pulled the wide doors open again.

The unicorn stood when light filtered to the center of the closet. Crystal stared at the animal. He stared back with dazzling green eyes, the only part of him that was beautiful.

"Why are you so ugly?" Crystal blurted out.

"Why are you so rude?" he answered.

Crystal's cheeks grew warm. "I've always thought that unicorns were pretty."

The creature snorted and coughed. Crystal covered her nose. And she thought her Labrador had bad breath!

"Unicorns who are loved, worshipped, and admired are beautiful, it's true. But when I came here to your world, as all unicorns must, I discovered that most humans don't believe in us anymore. Your world has changed since the stories my great-grandmare told us colts, stories of awestruck humans who waited for a glimpse of a unicorn, and believed even if that chance never came."

"I'm too old for fairy tales," Crystal said. At least, that's what she'd been told. Her mother insisted it was time for her to focus on school and making friends, instead of daydreaming and telling tales. As Janna had reminded her, it was time to grow up.

The unicorn cleared his throat. "Each of my kind must leave the safety of Unicorn Forest when our horns have turned from the silver of infancy to the gold of maturing youth. We must find those who would believe in us before we can return home. It is our legacy, to return with the magic of human belief, our true power."

Crystal moved closer, unable to look away from the unicorn's eyes. "Are there many? Unicorns, I mean."

He closed his eyes. Crystal wanted to ask him to open them again.

"There were once hundreds of unicorns, roaming in and out of your world and mine. So few are left now, perhaps a dozen. Many never returned, fading away when unable to find a human to believe in them. I have searched and found none in this time who truly want to believe. If I don't go home soon, I'll die. It is our way."

Crystal heard the sadness drip from the creature's words. "But if I can see you, why can't anyone else?"

"Because you are creative, imaginative . . ."

"I'm a liar," Crystal said.

The unicorn shook his head. "I've chosen you."

"Me? For what?"

"To help the others believe."

Crystal laughed. "You've chosen the wrong person. No one believes anything I say. I once told them that I was asked to be the first kid in a wheelchair on the space shuttle. I've told them I'm a secret agent, waiting for the right moment to jump up and catch the principal, who is really a spy on vacation. I've told them a dragon lives in my head and tells me what to say."

"I know." The unicorn tossed his head until his stringy mane stood out on his neck like an old mop. "But wouldn't you like to be believed? After all, you really have seen me, and even your best friend didn't believe you."

Crystal frowned and folded her arms. "So what? I've never cared before whether they believed anything I've said."

"Haven't you? What about the rodeo? And winning the grand prize trophy?"

Crystal gasped. How could he know about that? It was the first thing she'd told everyone when she moved to town. No one had believed her, even when she showed them the trophy and the photo of her uncle's horse. "You could have bought it and had it engraved," they had said.

She'd told whoppers ever since.

"Well, I need to be believed in, too," the unicorn said, stomping his hoof against the floor. "Help me."

Crystal studied the unicorn. Even in his ugliness he had a graceful quality, looking like something between a horse and a goat. She remembered how she'd felt when riding the horse in the rodeo. Fast and free, no wheelchair. Most of all, she remembered how much it had hurt when no one had believed she won the trophy.

"Okay, I'll try, but I can't make any promises." As soon as she agreed, Crystal wondered why she'd said the words. She met the unicorn's eyes again, then blinked and looked away. "How am I supposed to get them to believe if they can't see you?"

"When they believe, they'll see me."

Crystal groaned. They would only see the unicorn if they believed, but she had no idea how she'd get them to believe without seeing him.

"That's ridiculous," she said aloud.

"Go home," the unicorn whispered. "I'll be waiting for you. Sometimes you have to take things one step, one person at a time. I have chosen you to help me. I can only ask for help from a human one time. You are my only chance."

Crystal rolled away, glanced at the unicorn once more, then pushed the doors closed. She went outside and was glad to see that Janna hadn't gone home yet. They waited in silence for their rides.

"I'm sorry, Crystal. It's just that when you started saying . . ." Janna began.

Crystal looked into her friend's eyes. "I really saw him, Janna, I really did."

Janna looked away as if the words hadn't been spoken. "Did I tell you Mom took me to the mall last night to get that new CD we've been wanting? Ask your parents if you can sleep over tonight."

"Sure," Crystal mumbled.

She wished she'd never promised that mangy old unicorn to help him. By Monday, she'd be known as the "weirdo who saw unicorns in supply closets." Especially with Tracey's big mouth. It wasn't fair. Crystal didn't *ask* him to just show up and give her an impossible quest. How could she convince the kids that there really was a unicorn in the supply closet, and that if they only believed, they would see him?

All weekend, Crystal thought about the supply closet and the unicorn inside, sitting alone.

She thought about him when she told her little sister that a kid in ragged clothes came knocking at the door, wanting only a princess doll for her very own. She thought about the unicorn when she slipped the princess doll, with its newly broken porcelain head, into the back of her closet. She thought about him every time she was tempted to lie, and did it anyway.

Early Monday morning, Crystal rushed to the auditorium. She expected to find the supply closet locked. It was open . . . as if waiting for her.

"Hello," she said when the unicorn opened his eyes and yawned.

The creature looked past her. His head drooped. "I was hoping to see you surrounded by others."

Crystal shook her head. "I tried to tell Janna Friday night, but she ignored me." She saw that the unicorn's hair looked gray. His horn was beginning to crack. Even his eyes weren't as bright as before. "No one at school will ever believe me, I've told too many stories."

A single tear slid from the unicorn's eye. "Then I'll just turn into dust and disappear."

"How much time do you have?"

"We are given a year in your world to receive the magic of belief. My year ends with the new moon."

"But . . . it's almost full," she cried, gripping the arms of the wheelchair. "I believe in you! Isn't that enough?"

"I let you see me, Crystal. I can only do that once. Now, I must depend on you."

"Oh, please, let me try again. I'll find a way."

The unicorn blinked. "Would you like to ride a unicorn? Do you wish to see my home?"

"Oh, yes," Crystal said.

"Then touch my horn and climb upon my back."

He bent his head forward. Crystal reached out and touched the twisted horn. Her finger tingled. The tingling spread to her hand, her arm, and down her legs. She grasped the side of the wheelchair and stood.

A cry escaped her lips as she took two steps to the unicorn. He knelt on the dusty floor for her to slip onto his back.

"Close your eyes," he said.

"But . . . I thought you can't go home until others believe."

The unicorn seemed to sigh. "I have enough strength to make one thought-journey. Now close your eyes and do not open them until I tell you."

Crystal shut her eyes. She saw herself on the unicorn's back, bursting out of the closet. They moved through the school, as if pushed by an unseen wind, until they were outside.

Crystal clutched the creature's mane. She opened her eyes and saw only the supply closet, her empty wheelchair waiting in the doorway. Quickly she squeezed her eyes shut again and felt the vision embrace her. It was like watching a video, except that she could see, hear, and smell everything.

They sped past buildings and roads, across meadows and over hills. *No one will ever believe this.* She stared down at the world below them as it slid away in a veil of mist.

"There! Ahead lies Unicorn Forest," the unicorn shouted.

Crystal watched the foggy outline of the trees grow

taller as they approached. The mist thinned, then melted like snow. The unicorn landed with a gentle bump and walked into the forest. The trees seemed to glow, as if darkness never dared invade such a place.

Crystal twisted and turned, watching for the healthy unicorns that must live in the quiet wooded grove. Once or twice she glimpsed what she thought was the tip of a horn spiraling from behind a tree, or the sparkling glint of a snow-white tail. But then it was gone, leaving only the shadows cast from windblown branches.

"It's wonderful," Crystal whispered. "But where are the unicorns?" She glanced around, suddenly sure this was nothing more than an ordinary forest made magical by her imagination and the unicorn's dreams.

"They are around you, the last few who remain," the unicorn said.

"Then why can't I see them?"

The unicorn turned his head to look at her with one emerald eye. "They aren't yours to see."

Crystal's eyes widened. "Are you mine to see? Were you given to me?"

The unicorn snickered softly as if laughing at the thought. "I *chose* you."

Crystal lay her head against the unicorn's head. *I chose you.* That was the third time he'd said those words to her.

She ran her fingers through his coarse hair and wondered how it would feel if the others believed in him, too.

Would he really become beautiful? Would it matter? He was, after all, a real unicorn. And who was she to say that all unicorns had to be the same.

Too quickly, they left the forest and returned to the school. Crystal opened her eyes. She slid from the unicorn's back and hurried to her wheelchair as her legs weakened. She remembered reading once that if you touched the horn of a unicorn, you would be healed.

"Can you make me walk again?" she asked.

He shook his head. "I'm sorry, but that isn't the healing you need the most."

"But . . ."

The unicorn sighed as his eyes closed. Crystal backed away and shut the closet doors.

That night in bed, she thought about all the stories she'd told over the last few months. No wonder her classmates wouldn't believe her. But maybe, maybe if she started telling the truth . . .

She didn't tell one lie all week. When she sat beside Janna in the cafeteria, she admitted, "I lied to you last week when you wanted to go to the mall. I didn't have to wait for the television repairman. I was grounded."

Janna's eyes widened. "Wow, you're really telling the truth?"

Crystal smiled.

That week, Crystal admitted every lie she'd ever told anyone in school—at least, the ones she remembered. She even apologized to Mr. Wells in English. "I really didn't give my book report to a kid who couldn't read. I forgot to do it."

Mr. Wells nodded. "I know, but thank you for being honest. Storytelling is a special ability, but only when you know the difference between reality and make-believe."

Crystal thought she was beginning to understand.

She had one more story to tell everyone.

She got her chance Friday after school when the Drama Club met to give their soliloquies.

Crystal watched them fill the front row of the auditorium, and her stomach filled with butterflies. What if everyone laughed at her when she talked? If the kids didn't believe her, the unicorn would just turn into dust. She couldn't let it happen, not when this was her chance to give him the magic he needed.

Please let them believe me. This time, it's important.

She couldn't keep her eyes off the closet as the others went onstage. When her turn came, Crystal moved past the stage, stopped, and opened the supply closet doors. She lost herself in the unicorn's eyes for a moment, then turned her wheelchair to face the others.

Mrs. Gray motioned for her to go to the microphone, but Crystal ignored her.

Without an explanation, she began to describe the Unicorn Forest. At first there were giggles and groans and whispers of "Uh-oh, she's starting again."

Then her voice grew louder and confident as she told of the wondrous things she'd seen. She described the unicorn and his need for their belief. She told them every-thing she saw and felt as she flew upon the unicorn's back, and how the forest seemed alive with hidden magic, a magic waiting for anyone who believed.

Crystal could see it in their eyes, as one by one they leaned forward to listen to her story, then, one by one looked past her and pointed toward the open supply closet.

When Crystal stopped talking, Tracey Hammond stood.

"Oh, look, it really *is* a unicorn," she whispered. She stared at Crystal. "I'm sorry I didn't believe. He's so beautiful."

Crystal's heart fell. Beautiful? Were they only pretend-ing to see the unicorn? She rolled forward, then turned her wheelchair to face the closet.

The closet glowed with the brightness of the unicorn's dazzling white coat. His mane rippled when he moved his head, and the horn was a spiral of gold sprouting from his forehead.

Crystal groaned. Had *her* unicorn faded away before she helped her friends believe? She looked into the ani-mal's stunning green eyes. The unicorn winked.

It *was* him! Crystal took a deep breath and grinned as Tracey stood and moved closer to touch the unicorn. Others followed her. Crystal knew that before long, the whole school would come to the auditorium to visit the unicorn in the supply closet, and his magic would grow.

Crystal watched them a moment, then rolled up the

ramp to the center of the stage. She leaned forward into the microphone.

"Hey!"

Everyone turned toward her.

"I once knew a dragon that lived in my head. He whispered stories in my ears and I told them to everyone."

Her classmates stared, some nodding as if ready to believe her now. Crystal smiled. "But the dragon doesn't live there anymore, he went away when the unicorn brought me a true story."

The unicorn laughed. Crystal turned off the mike and blew a kiss to the horned creature. Sometimes a dragon was just a story. And sometimes, there really were unicorns in supply closets.

CHILD OF FAERIE

~ GAIL KIMBERLY ~

Afton was the only one who ever swam at this end of Wicca Lake. It was weedy and shallow, so the other kids went to the cove, where there was a sandy beach and rafts.

But Afton liked to come here alone. Then the dryads who lived in the tree hollows would tell her the latest news of Faerie, or the moss maidens would climb down from their nests in the branches to share the bee-bread and nectar they'd brought back. She envied them. They were all so tiny they could use the space-time pinholes to come and go as they pleased.

On this hot summer afternoon, as Afton splashed in the cool green water, she saw the unicorn.

Sunlight dappled his brilliant white coat with leaf-shadows as he trotted to the edge of the lake and gazed at her, his eyes deep blue and glowing. The single horn on his forehead shone ice-white and his silvery mane and tail shimmered with rainbow glints.

Surprised, Afton cried out, "Corandell!" and splashed quickly to the shore.

I knew I'd recognize you, even in human form, his thoughts told her. *You haven't grown much bigger, and you still have your black hair and Faerie eyes.*

She hugged his graceful neck and caught the scent of meadow grass and sandalwood on his mane. "I've missed you so much!"

We've all missed you, too. Climb on my back and come home with me now.

The space-time window must be open again. The one big enough for her and the unicorn to go through.

"Oh, Corandell, I can't. Not right now!"

Why not? You promised your parents you'd come back soon, remember? When you were curious about Earth they let you come here, but only for a visit. You've stayed more than a year.

Had it really been a whole Faerie year? Of course, it must have been. She had come to Earth in the form of a human infant and she was thirteen now. The time had passed so quickly, she hadn't realized.

"My other father has been sick and the family needs me," Afton told him.

Humans get sick and die, Afton. If you stay here, you will grow old and die, too.

"It will be many more Earth years before I'm old, Corandell. But I won't stay that long. I just can't leave right now." She knew that Faerie time moved so slowly, her mother, father, and two brothers would still be young and unchanged when she returned to them.

Corandell's stern gaze made her uncomfortable. But she couldn't desert her human family without preparing them, somehow. She loved them, and they had loved her ever since they'd found her as a baby on their doorstep. Now Mom and Dad thought of her as their daughter, and she and Rachel were like real sisters.

"When the window opens again, after the third new moon, I'll be ready," she told Corandell. "Come for me then."

I don't want to frighten you, child, but it might never open again. It stayed closed for the last four moons and no one knows why. Even your mother's magic has no power to open it. Corandell's sapphire eyes were troubled. *When I came through today it was only about half open. There's no way to tell if it will stay open even that much for the usual two days.*

She stared at him, alarmed. It would be awful to be stranded here forever—to never see Faerie or her family there again. She'd always known Corandell would come for her one day. Why hadn't she prepared herself?

Climb on my back, Afton. The window could close at any moment and never open again! He nudged her arm urgently, his horn flashing pale colors.

He was so beautiful, she thought, but pallid here compared to the magnificence he had in Faerie. Everything else here—colors, music, fragrances—seemed duller, too.

She should just leap on his back right now and let him take her home.

But her human family and friends would be heartbroken, never knowing what had happened to her. They didn't know where she came from or that she had to return. She had to think of some way to tell them she was going away and that she'd be all right.

"I need just a little more time to get ready," she told Corandell. "I'll go with you tomorrow."

And what if the window closes today?

Afton hoped with all her heart that it wouldn't, but she knew what she had to do. "Go back to Faerie, Corandell. If the window isn't open tomorrow, come for me when it opens again, whenever that might be."

It might never be. He tossed his head impatiently. *Afton, come with me now. Your parents are lonely since your brothers are both on a quest for a lost princess of Elfland. Then remember you have to lead the dancers in the midsummer ball. And Prince Roland is pining for you.*

A piece of her heart tore, remembering her other life. She put her hand against the ache. "All right. Tell my parents I love them and I'm coming home. But not today. I'll be here to meet you at sunset tomorrow."

The unicorn gazed at her sorrowfully, then suddenly turned and raced toward two weeping willows by the edge of the lake. She watched as he passed between the two trees that must be the portal to the space-time window. In a moment he disappeared in the mist that rose to envelop him.

Dark clouds were gathering now and a chilly breeze was blowing. Sadly, Afton pulled her shorts and shirt over her wet swimsuit and headed for her parents' farm.

Rachel was in the pasture with Peg, feeding the old horse sugar cubes from a plastic bag. Seeing her nine-year-old sister, Afton wanted to cry. They'd had such good times together. She'd always remember picnicking in the woods in summer and skating on the frozen pond in winter. She'd remember the beautiful songs Rachel composed and sang in her pretty, warbling voice while Afton accompanied her on Dad's old guitar. And how she would tell Rachel stories about Faerie and its inhabitants, even about the moss maidens and dryads who lived by Wicca Lake. Rachel loved to hear the tales and at first Afton pretended she was making them up. After a while Rachel said the Faerie world sounded so enchanting, she wanted to believe it was real.

Afton didn't have a sister in Faerie. She would miss Rachel very much.

"I tried to ride Peg to the meadow," Rachel told her, "but she's going lame. I had to get off."

"Well, she *is* old." Afton stroked Peg's balding, white-and-brown back. It felt thin and scruffy after Corandell's satiny coat. "I noticed that stiff leg, too. We'll give her a rest and maybe it will get better." She hoped so. She and Rachel had loved to ride Peg ever since they were little, Afton sometimes imagining she was riding Corandell again.

"I took her right back to the barn, Afton, but there's nothing there to feed her." Rachel reached into the bag for another sugar cube. "I looked all over but couldn't find any oats or hay or anything. So I brought her out here to graze."

"That's strange! We'd better tell Mom and Dad." Afton looked up at the dark sky. "It's going to rain, but she'll be okay here."

They ran through the barnyard, scattering noisy chickens, and into the farmhouse through the kitchen door.

Mom was there, busy among the delicious smells of pot roast and baking bread. Afton noticed how tired she looked. She'd been nervous and worried ever since Dad's heart attack.

Mom ran her hand through her short copper curls, so like Rachel's. "You girls stay close. There's a storm coming."

Afton shrugged. "It's only the Wind Folletti throwing rain clouds at each other."

"Wind *what*?" Mom looked puzzled.

"Folletti. They're nasty little imps. They travel in small whirls of wind and try to do as much damage as they can."

"I don't know where you get these wild stories, Afton!" Mom shook her head, smiling. "Will you fix a green salad for supper? Rachel, you can set the table."

Afton took the wooden salad bowl out of the cupboard. She could never tell Mom and Dad the truth about having to go back to Faerie. They'd always teased her about having too much imagination. Maybe she should leave them a note with some made-up explanation. She could say she was running away to live in another state. No, then they'd worry and try to find her.

"We were looking for hay or oats to feed Peg," Rachel told Mom, "but there isn't anything for her in the barn. Can we go to town tomorrow and get some?"

Mom frowned at the potato she was peeling. Then she put it and the peeler on the counter and wiped her hands on her worn jeans. "Both of you better come with me."

Puzzled, the girls followed her into Dad's office, where he sat hunched over a big ledger on his desk. Dad couldn't do any hard work since he'd had that heart attack. The hired man had to do everything for him now. But Dad said he still had to keep his eye on things.

He pushed back his chair and smiled at them. "What are you girls up to?"

"They were asking about old Peg," Mom said. "I thought both of us should tell them."

"All right." Dad was suddenly solemn. "I guess you know we didn't make much money last year."

"But everybody says the corn crop should be good this year," Afton said.

Dad shook his head. "Everybody's just hoping. There's been too much rain. We can't afford to keep going any longer." He reached out and took Mom's hand. "Your mother and I have decided to sell the farm."

"We'll move to Saginaw," Mom said cheerfully. "It will be easier for Dad there. And you girls will like living in the city. There are good schools and lots of interesting things to see and do."

"But I don't want to move!" Rachel wailed.

"It's not as though we won't ever come back," Mom told her. "We'll come visit Grandma and Grandpa often."

Afton was stunned. If the space-time window closed today, how would she know if it opened again? Could Corandell find her in the city? She should have gone with him. Now she might never be able to go home.

At dinner, Rachel only stared sadly at her food. Afton found she couldn't eat, either. Finally, Mom insisted they take at least a few bites, and while the thunder rumbled and the rain knocked on the kitchen windows, their parents talked about the exciting things they might do when they moved to the city.

Then Afton remembered. "What about Peg?"

Mom shook her head sorrowfully. "We can't take her with us."

"Are you going to sell her, too?" Rachel looked anxious.

A sad, sick feeling overwhelmed Afton. "Nobody's going to buy a horse that old, Rachel. They're going to have to put her down."

Rachel looked at her parents, horrified. "You don't mean that, do you?"

Dad looked away from her. "None of us want to do it, Rachel, but we have to face reality. Peg's old. She's going lame and she's almost blind. She won't live much longer anyway. We all have to go sometime."

And I have to go, too, Afton thought miserably. Just like Peg. Only I have to figure out how to leave you. And how will Rachel feel, losing both of us?

After dinner the two girls took Peg back to the barn, and when their parents were in bed, they sneaked out to spend the night there. They carried a big flashlight, their blankets and pillows, and a box of oat cereal and three apples for Peg. They stroked her and told her what a good old girl she was, then they lay awake talking about what they might do to save her.

"There has to be somebody who'll take care of her," Rachel said.

But they couldn't think of anyone.

Then Afton sat up, exultant. "I know what we can do! We'll hide her in the woods by the lake. I know a place where nobody ever goes, except the dryads and moss maidens. I'll ask them to look after her."

"Don't tell stories *now*, Afton. This is serious."

"I *am* serious."

"And the dryads and moss maidens are really, really, real?"

"Of course. I thought you knew that. You told me you believed in them."

Rachel hesitated a moment before she answered. "I guess I do, but I've never *seen* them. How come you never take me with you when you go?"

"They're shy. They won't come out if anyone else is there."

"Even me?" Rachel sulked. "Then how come you think they'll look after Peg?"

"They're only shy with humans. Peg will be safe with them and there's lots of grass for her to eat."

"Should we take her tonight, so nobody will see us?" Rachel sounded suddenly excited. She pulled her arm out from under the blanket and pointed the flashlight at her watch. "It's after midnight."

"Let's wait until it gets a bit lighter, so we can see where we're going."

They huddled under their blankets, while the rain tapped on the roof and the night wind blew the scent of wet grass into the barn. Peg, in her stall, shifted and snorted.

"I can't sleep," Rachel said. "This straw is too scratchy. What'll we tell Mom and Dad when they notice Peg's gone?"

Afton sighed. "I don't know. We could say she ran away. Or we could just pretend we don't know anything about her. We'll think of something."

"I feel bad, lying to them. But we're doing the right thing, aren't we?"

"I hope so," Afton said.

As soon as the sky was pale with the first light of dawn, the two girls led Peg out to the road, keeping the flashlight pointed down in case Mom or Dad looked out a window. Then they went across the field into the woods.

It was still dark here among the trees. Rain dripped

from the leaves, soaking their pajamas. They heard
unfamiliar sounds and saw strange forms looming in
the dimness. Rachel was scared and whimpered at every
noise.

"You don't have to come with me," Afton told her.
"I'll walk you home and then take Peg by myself."

"No," Rachel said bravely. "I want to go, too. And I
want to meet some dryads or moss maidens. Then maybe
they'll know I'm your sister so they don't have to be shy
with me."

Finally Afton saw the clearing ahead of them. Early
sunlight sifting through the branches turned the raindrops
on the grass into a carpet of sparkling diamonds.

"Is this the place?" Rachel looked around. "Are they
here?"

"No, they live by the edge of the lake. I'll go ask them
to watch Peg."

"I'm coming with you," Rachel said, shivering.

The two girls led the limping horse through the trees
to the lake. Just as Afton had expected, the tiny creatures
didn't show themselves. But she knew they were watching
and listening. Instead of using mind-speak, she called to
them aloud, so Rachel could hear, telling them about Peg
and why she and Rachel had to bring her here to hide her.
"Please keep her from straying or trying to follow us back
to the farm," she finished.

For a moment the only answer was the call of a mourning dove. Then a little green face appeared from behind a
leaf. "We'll do as you and Rachel wish, Afton," the moss

maiden said in her tinkling voice. Then she vanished again.

Rachel was ecstatic. "I saw her! She knows me!"

And maybe when I'm back in Faerie, Afton thought, they'll carry my messages to you.

"We don't have to tie Peg up," she told Rachel when they led her back to the clearing. "We'll just leave the apples for her and go back home, so Mom and Dad will think we were in bed all night."

"Okay." Rachel lined up the three apples on a flat black rock. She put her arms around Peg's neck and laid her cheek against it. "Stay here, old girl. We'll come back when we can."

As she moved away, Rachel picked something shimmering from a low branch near the rock. "Afton! Look at this!" She held it up between her thumb and forefinger, the end of it touching the ground. "It looks like a silver thread and it's as long as I am!"

Afton moved closer to see.

"Who would be sewing something out here?" Rachel handed it to her.

Afton smiled. "It's a hair from Corandell's tail."

"Who's Corandell?"

"My unicorn. He must have snagged his tail on that branch."

"A unicorn?" Rachel asked, astonished. "A real unicorn? Does he live here, too?"

Afton shook her head. "He was only visiting. He

lives in another place, in another time." Should she tell Rachel now?

"Then how come you said he's *your* unicorn, Afton?"

"Because he's my friend. I used to live in that same place. He came to take me back there with him."

"Can I go, too?" Rachel was dancing with excitement, her wet pajama legs flapping.

Afton looked into her sister's blue eyes, putting both hands on her shoulders. "When I go, you have to stay here with Mom and Dad, Rachel. They need you."

Rachel's freckled face crumpled and tears welled in her eyes. "When are you going to come back?"

"Maybe some day."

Rachel gave her a wide-eyed, unbelieving stare, then threw her arms around Afton and clamped her in a damp embrace. "Don't go! I want you to stay here!"

Afton hugged her for a long moment while she fought back her own tears. Then she pushed Rachel firmly away. "The only place I'm going right now is back home. We have to hurry before Mom and Dad wake up. And promise you won't tell them about the unicorn. It's our secret."

"I promise." Rachel wiped her eyes. "But will you stay?"

"Remember what Dad said? We all have to go some-time." Afton looked thoughtfully at the old horse, who was nibbling one of the apples. Then she walked over to her, still holding the long hair, and looped it around her neck. "There," she said, tying the ends in a knot. "Now when Corandell comes back, he'll know you're our horse."

When they returned to the farm they collected their blankets and pillows from the barn and slipped into the house as quietly as they could. In their bedroom they changed their wet pajamas for dry ones and climbed into their twin beds. Rachel immediately fell asleep. In spite of her worry, Afton dozed.

They hadn't slept long before Mom woke them. "Dad and I are going to town to see about selling the farm," she told them. "We have to hurry for our appointment. We'll be gone most of the day. I know I can count on you, Afton, to stay with Rachel today and make the meals." She kissed Afton and hugged her. "I don't know what Dad and I would ever do without you!"

Then she went to Rachel's bed and kissed her. "You both look so sad! You're unhappy about Peg and about having to move, aren't you? I know it's hard for you. But just remember, everything's going to be fine as long as we have each other."

Rachel cried when they left. "How come we have to move?" she wailed. "And how come you're going away with that unicorn?"

Afton fought back her own tears. Her mother's words made her feel worse than ever, tearing her in two.

She gave Rachel her funniest book to cheer her up while she made breakfast, and afterward they kept busy gathering eggs and picking raspberries. When their chores were done, they played games until late afternoon. Then Afton went into Dad's office and wrote Mom and Dad a note. She realized she didn't want to make up a lie, so she told them the truth, and that she loved them and would never forget them.

When it was nearly sunset, she told Rachel she had to leave for a while, that she was going to see a friend.

"I want to go with you," Rachel's face was determined. "You're going to meet that unicorn, aren't you?"

"He might not even be there." But Afton knew her sister would only follow her. Maybe Rachel would feel better, understand better, if she saw Corandell. And when Afton was gone, if Rachel told Mom and Dad what she had seen, it could help them understand, too.

"All right," Afton said. "We'll go see how Peg is doing."

The sun was setting when they got to the clearing where they'd left the old horse.

But she wasn't there.

"Maybe she went to the lake to get a drink," Afton said.

They ran through the woods to the brink of the lake. Mallard ducks swam peacefully on the shallow water, their babies in neat rows behind them. Down by the beaver dam, the great blue heron stood on his long stick legs, watching for unwary fish. Peg was nowhere around.

"She can't be far away," Afton said, but she was worried. How could the moss maidens and dryads let Peg stray? And Corandell wasn't here, either. That must mean the window had closed.

"This is awful!" Rachel sobbed. "We've lost Peg!"

They started along the bank to look for her. Then Afton gave a wordless cry and pointed. Rachel shaded her eyes to see.

There, in the radiance of the setting sun, two animals were trotting out of the woods, side by side, one of them with a stiff leg.

"It *is* a unicorn!" Rachel's eyes were shining. "He's with Peg!"

Corandell came toward them, Peg limping after him.

Afton, are you ready to come with me now?

She glanced at Rachel who was gazing at him, awe-struck.

Corandell tossed his head and stomped impatiently. *You must get on my back. It's been two days. The window will close after us. No one knows when it will open again.*

But Afton still hesitated. "Can I take one of the hairs from your tail?"

All right, but hurry! He turned to let her pull out a long, silky thread.

Afton looped it several times around Rachel's wrist. "Now you're protected by Faerie magic."

Rachel looked at the silvery bracelet, then up at Afton. "Everything *won't* be all right, will it?" A tear rolled down her cheek. "Because we won't all be together." She threw her arms around Afton and clung to her.

Afton! Corandell's thoughts thundered. *Climb on my back!*

Afton held her sister close, feeling Rachel's pounding heart and her tears falling warm on her own neck. She thought of how Rachel would feel, going back home alone to an empty house, then trying to explain to Mom and Dad when they got home.

They would all have one more thing to grieve for. And so would she. How could she cause so much pain?

Now she knew what she had to do.

"I'd like to go with you but I can't," she told Corandell. "I'm going to stay here with my family."

Rachel drew back, astonished. "You will? Oh, Afton, I'm so glad!"

Seeing Rachel's happiness, the unicorn's azure eyes gleamed sorrowfully. *Aren't you forgetting your other family? They love you, too, Afton. They want you back, and so do I.*

"My Earth family needs me. Dad lost his good health. They're losing their farm and their way of life. I can't let them lose me, too."

So much sadness here and you still want to stay?

"Yes."

Then you must be doing the right thing. But I'll come for you again some day, Afton. Perhaps they won't always need you as much as they do now.

Afton threw her arms around Corandell's neck and hugged him. He nuzzled her cheek, then turned away and trotted toward the two weeping willows near the lake's edge.

"Wait!" Afton called. She grabbed Peg's bridle, leading the horse to where Corandell stood. "You said two of you can get through the window?"

Corandell turned his gaze toward Peg. Then he nodded. *Yes. Of course she can come with me. She will love the woods and meadows of Faerie.*

The unicorn nudged the old horse so that she went between the willows, and followed her through the portal. Then, suddenly, they were running together into a rising mist, Peg moving as swiftly and gracefully, now, as she used to, her sleek brown-and-white coat catching the sun's red reflection.

The two girls watched them until they disappeared.

THE
NEW GIRL

— SEAN STEWART —

There was a new girl coming to groom the unicorn. He didn't much like the look of her. She
was skinny and plain and she slouched. Her
straight brown hair was short and ragged, as if whoever
cut it didn't care what it looked like. An old dress of her
mother's was hitched around her waist with a twine belt.
More dirty twine tied a pair of men's boots tight around
her ankles.

She was carrying a comb and a shovel. She tossed the
shovel over the outer fence and then let herself in the first
gate and stood for a moment, looking at the unicorn. "It
smells the same," she said.

He didn't answer.

"Your manure. Smells just like a horse's. I was hoping
it would be different."

"Where's Polly?" he said.

"Oh well, no surprise, really." The girl closed the first

gate behind her, locked it, and stood the shovel against the inner fence.

"I don't want you in here. Your manners are bad and you haven't washed this morning." His great eyes narrowed. "And you've kissed a boy. I can smell it."

She opened the inner gate. "And I'd have done it again, if he'd been worth it. But don't worry: The boys in this village are all clods. Dumb as turnips, every one." She closed the gate behind her, and latched it. "My name's Meg."

"I know your name. It's a small village."

"No kidding."

"Polly had beautiful manners. She always washed and she had some respect. Please tell the mayor I wish to have her back."

"See, there's something we both want," Meg said. She looked around the unicorn's enclosure: crude wooden trough, bales of old hay next to it. At the far side, a dirty canvas canopy in case he wanted to get out of the rain or snow. And all around, the high wooden fence, like a dingy mockery of the mountains ringing little Lammerton Vale. "I didn't cheer when they told me I had another stall to shovel out. But pretty blond Polly is gone, you see. She ran off with a soldier last night. Didn't even leave a note. Her brother Mick's chasing after them to try and fetch her back. Don't wager on it, I say. I say she's gone for good."

"Gone?" The unicorn remembered the morning they had met, Polly coming into the high meadow, a slip of a girl then, no more than nine, and the innocence in her eyes. She had snared his heart at that moment, long before she whispered her secrets in his ear and laid her bridle on his neck.

Plain dirty Meg shrugged, her face hard. "Quite the lass, Polly was. Yours isn't the only broken heart in Lammerton this morning."

The next morning came dark and cold. Winter was on its way. Somewhere behind the mountains the sun had come up, but it would be another two hours before they saw it, tucked down here in the valley. Meg was wearing the same clothes when she came to the unicorn's paddock: the worn felt shirt, the too-big dress, her father's cast-off boots. She let herself through the outer gate, then turned and latched it behind her. "Polly's brother Mick is back, did you hear?"

"Yes. They brought him to me to be healed."

"They say the soldier's friends snapped him into kindling," Meg said. "Will he live?"

"Yes." Mick had gone into shock by the time they carried him to the paddock in the middle of the night. The touch of the unicorn's breath had stopped the bleeding inside, but the young man's jaw and hip had been badly broken.

"Will he be lame?" Meg said.

"Probably."

"Will he be ugly?"

The unicorn didn't answer.

"Some sister," Meg said.

"She didn't know."

"Were you there?" Meg said. She let herself through the inner gate, kicked it closed, dumped her broom and comb, and latched the gate behind her. "No. You were here in your cage."

"Polly would never have let them hurt Mick if she had known."

Meg clasped her small, hard, dirty hands over her heart. "Ah, his love is gone, but his horsey heart still is true."

The unicorn looked at her. "Does it make you so angry, that Polly was prettier than you?"

Meg colored.

"Or did you want that soldier for yourself? Did you love the way he looked in his fine red coat?"

"I don't give a snapped straw for the soldier and neither did she," Meg said furiously. "He was a way *out*, you see? A way out of Lammerton, and seeing the same two dozen people at church every Sunday, and talking about the weather, and pulling eggs out of hens until they don't lay enough and wringing their necks after, and taking care of your mother who's either drunk or crying."

"Polly's mother doesn't drink," the unicorn said.

"Shut up."

Meg mucked out the unicorn's paddock. Then she took the big currying comb and starting brushing his mane.

"Polly would not have left if she didn't love him," the unicorn said.

"You have another big day ahead of you," Meg said, brushing hard. Each stroke stung his flanks but he held still. "There's an archery meet over in Copsfield today. The men will be down after breakfast to touch their bows to your horn for good fortune. Maybe, if you're lucky, they'll take you along to be their mascot. I might even have to braid a ribbon in your tail." Meg spat. "You came to Lammerton for love," she said. She looked around the little paddock with its double gate and canvas canopy, the wooden trough and the apple tree branches, naked now with winter coming. "Look where it got you."

Meg slipped through the gates very quietly the next morning, looking at the ground. There was another loop of twine holding her left boot together, and she wore a greasy sweater over the felt shirt.

It was a dull November day, cloudy and spitting with small cold rain. Meg mucked out the unicorn's paddock in silence. Then he stood under the canopy at the back of the corral while she brushed his coat. "Sorry about yesterday," she said.

"It's been hard since your father left," the unicorn said gently.

The brush stopped on his flank. "How did you know?"

"Polly told me. We used to talk a lot."

"Ah." The brush began to move again. "It is a small village, isn't it."

"Polly said he went to the city to seek his fortune."

The rain picked up, drumming on the canvas canopy and dripping from its edges into the muddy paddock.

"What is it like to be free?" Meg asked. "Where you were before Polly found you, up in the mountains? Is it beautiful?"

"Yes." The unicorn felt her against his flank, one hand pulling the comb, the other following after, stroking his mane. The bones in her thin forearms. The warmth of her. "It is very beautiful, and very cold. The mountain streams are like cold wet sunshine. The eagles fly with all wild creation under their wings."

"Were you lonely?"

"No. Not then."

"Would you be, if you went back now?"

"I don't know," the unicorn said.

"No one to brush out your mane," Meg said. "No one to put a pretty ribbon in your tail." She grinned, just a little. "It's not so bad, being a pet."

He flinched, a tremor going through his powerful shoulders.

A silence. "Sorry. That was mean."

"It's true," he said.

Meg finished currying his tail and bent to check his hooves. She didn't have Polly's gentle touch and her hands were hard, but they were sure. "You've handled a lot of stock," the unicorn said.

"Had to, since Dad . . . you know."

He raised his rear right hock for inspection. "I think there's a pebble in this one."

"Yeah." Meg pulled a clasp knife from her pocket and dug the stone out with it. "There."

"Polly wouldn't have done that, you know. She would have called the farrier."

Meg dropped the hoof. "She wouldn't want to hurt you."

She stayed there for a minute, squatting on the ground, not looking at him. "You know what? I don't blame Dad. Not one tinker's spit. I'd have left us, too, if I were him. I suppose that makes me a terrible daughter."

"It's not wrong to want to be free," the unicorn said gently.

When Meg was sad her mouth turned down at the corners and made her look ugly. "Isn't it wrong to walk out on the people who count on you? What about them? What about the ones left behind? What about the ones who *can't* just choose to be free? Should I run off with some brute in a red coat so I don't have to watch my mother drink herself to death? Or do I stay in Lammerton and watch the sky get smaller and smaller until I'm too old and scared to leave?" Meg was crying. "I am so scared. I am so scared of being alone."

He let her cry. When she was done she wiped the tears away with the back of her dirty hand, smearing mud on her cheeks. "Why are you being so nice to me, anyway?"

"I love," the unicorn said. "It's what I do."

That night she came back. From far down the meadow he saw her yellow lantern swinging, startling the crows. The rain had stopped, but the clouds remained and there were no stars. The night had turned cold. Ice crept over the puddles where the rain had filled his hoofprints. As she came closer, he could hear the grass, stiff with frost, brushing against the hem of her skirt.

She held the lantern low and close to her body, where it would light her way without being seen by any villagers up late. She put it down next to the outer gate, facing away from Lammerton. She blew on her cold hands and rubbed them together before lifting the latch and pushing the outer gate open. The cold wood squeaked and she froze. A moment passed, and then she slid inside.

She left the outer gate open and unlatched.

"It's freezing," Meg said. Her breath smoked in the cold air. "You should be under the canopy."

"This is a summer's day to what I've seen in the mountains. Nights I've stood on a ridge no man has named and the wind has come like winter's breath. The stars like ice broken across the sky."

"I can't leave Mum," Meg said. "Not now. Not even soon."

"You can't take care of her forever."

Meg raised one eyebrow. "This from the beast that gave up his life to wink good luck on babies' birthdays? To nod his horn as a charm for a good harvest of pumpkins or a nice barrel of beer?"

"What if your mother is still alive when you have

grown into a woman? Will you leave then, or will you stay here in Lammerton?"

The thin winter wind made Meg's bangs flutter like rags on a washing line. "I don't know. Someday I'll leave, though. I swear it to you."

"Where will you go?"

"The city, I suppose. Like Dad." Meg shivered and blew on her hands again. "I'm not cut out for the mountains. Too lonely, there." She pressed her hands against her ears. "Lord, it's cold out tonight. I told Mum I was off to the outhouse. Even in her cups she'll miss me if I'm not back soon."

She backed out of the paddock, leaving both gates open and unlatched.

He looked at her. "Aren't you forgetting something?"

Slowly, Meg shook her head. "I don't think so."

He followed her to the edge of the fence. "I don't want you to get in trouble."

She shrugged. "I'm always in trouble."

"I'm not surprised," he said. She grinned.

Meg stooped to pick up her lamp. Shadows jumped and swayed on the cold ground. "Live," she whispered fiercely to him. "Be free."

She turned as if to hurry off, but stopped. With her back to him she said, "Will I ever see you again?"

"Do you want to?"

"Yes. Even if it's only once. Even if it's not until I'm old and living in the city and about to die, I want to see you again. Can I?"

"I don't know."

"That's hard." She shivered, facing the great dark mountains. "I can love, too, you know."

She felt the touch of his breath on the back of her neck, warm as summer, but she didn't dare look back and let him see her crying.

"I know," he said.

ABOUT THE
AUTHORS

NANCY VARIAN Berberick lives in Charlotte, North Carolina, where she likes to garden and hike with her husband, Bruce, and their dog, Pagie. She has written numerous fantasy novels and short stories for adults. Her books include *The Panther's Hoard*, *Stormblade*, and *The Jewels of Elvish*.

BRUCE COVILLE has published over sixty books for young readers, including *Goblins in the Castle*, the MY TEACHER IS AN ALIEN series, and the picture book *Sarah's Unicorn*, which was illustrated by his wife, Katherine. He is currently working on the second installment in THE UNICORN CHRONICLES, a series of novels about Luster, the unicorn world featured in his story for this book.

KATHERINE COVILLE has illustrated over two dozen books for young readers, including *Space Brat*, *The World's Worst*

Fairy Godmother, and *Sarah's Unicorn*. This is her first published story. Katherine enjoys making miniatures, and once turned an acorn into a doll house. She lives in Syracuse, New York with her husband, Bruce; their youngest son, Adam; and more pets than are really necessary.

ALETHEA EASON is a reading specialist in an elementary school in Northern California. She has a deep interest in comparative religion and metaphysical studies. Alethea has published numerous poems, and three other stories. She is proud to note that a key idea for her story in this book came from Cody, one of her fifth-grade students.

GAIL KIMBERLY has been writing since she was seven, but it was many years before her first book, a science fiction novel titled *Flyer*, was published. Since then Gail has published eleven other books and many short stories, mostly science fiction and fantasy. Originally from Canada, she now lives with her husband, Kellin, in Brea, California, sharing the house and yard with four cats and one elderly dog.

GREG LABARBERA lives in Charlotte, North Carolina, with his wife, Jackie, and their three black Labradors. When he's not writing, Greg can be found teaching elementary school physical education, playing guitar with his rock band, or indulging his passion for rock climbing. He met his collaborator, Nancy Varian Berberick, in a writers' group.

KATHRYN LAY has had over 260 pieces published in such places as *Marion Zimmer Bradley's Fantasy Magazine*, *Boys' Life*, and *Highlights*. She loves to read, quilt, and make up stories. She has yet to find any unicorns in her closet, but declares she would believe in them if she did. Kathryn lives in Bedford, Texas, with her husband, daughter, two dogs, and a fish.

GREGORY MAGUIRE was born and raised in Albany, New York. He has published ten children's novels, including *Seven Spiders Spinning* and *Six Haunted Hairdos*, both part of his series THE HAMLET CHRONICLES. His adult novel, *Wicked*, tells the life story of the Wicked Witch of the West, famous from L. Frank Baum's *The Wizard of Oz*. A world traveler, Gregory currently lives in Concord, Massachusetts.

RUTH O'NEILL grew up in British Columbia. When she was five years old she tried to fly with wings made of construction paper. Fortunately, the tallest thing she could climb was a mailbox, so she only skinned her palms. However, the urge to fly clearly stuck with her, since she married her husband, Charles, while floating through the sky in a hot-air balloon. Currently she works for a software company as a systems analyst and watches "Pinky and the Brain" to relax.

JESSICA AMANDA SALMONSON has published a half-dozen novels and "a gazillion" short stories, which have garnered her the World Fantasy Award, the Lambda Award, the ReaderCon Award, and numerous appearances in "year's best" anthologies. Jessica's stepmother was a Buddhist priestess raised in a monastery in Thailand, which probably helps account for how many of Jessica's stories and novels have an Asian influence. She lives in Seattle.

JANNI LEE SIMNER grew up on Long Island but journeyed west as soon as she could, eventually finding her way to the Arizona desert. She now lives in Tucson, where she enjoys exploring the surrounding mountains, both on foot and on horseback. Her stories have appeared in over two dozen magazines and anthologies; her PHANTOM RIDER series features three books about a magical horse.

Texas-based SEAN STEWART is the author of several adult science fiction and fantasy novels, including *Passion Play* and *Clouds End*; readers who liked "The New Girl" might try his award-winning novel, *Nobody's Son*. Sean has two daughters and is still madly in love with the woman he began courting fifteen years ago.